Girls Like Us

Girls Like Us

RANDI PINK

FEIWEL AND FRIENDS

NEW YORK

An imprint of Macmillan Publishing Group, LLC
120 Broadway, New York, NY 10271
fiercereads.com

Our books may be purchased in bulk for promotional, educational, or business use.
Please contact your local bookseller or the Macmillan Corporate and Premium Sales
Department at (800) 221-7945 ext. 5442 or by email at
MacmillanSpecialMarkets@macmillan.com.

Library of Congress Cataloging-in-Publication Data is available.
ISBN 978-1-250-62087-3 (paperback) / ISBN 978-1-250-15586-3 (ebook)

Originally published in the United States by Feiwel and Friends
First Square Fish edition, 2021
Book designed by Katie Klimowicz
Square Fish logo designed by Filomena Tuosto

1 3 5 7 9 10 8 6 4 2

Mom

Not.

Once.

Not when I fell. Failed. Flunked out.

Not when I thought I was done living. Learning. Loving.

Not even when I broke your precious heart.

Not once have you doubted me.

Not.

Once.

This one's for you, My Love.

OLA AND IZELLA

11 Weeks & 6 Days Along

Summer 1972

Evangelist, Ola, and Izella formed a tight assembly line in their tiny kitchen. Evangelist shelled the peas, sixteen-year-old Ola bagged them into perfect portions, and fifteen-year-old Izella organized them by date in the deep freeze. Izella hated being the youngest. Always stuck with the easiest jobs—organize the vegetables, lay out the spoons, wipe down the table. She wanted to cut, strain, mix, and bake like her big sister, Ola, did from time to time, but Evangelist wouldn't allow it.

"Quit daydreaming, Babygal," Evangelist snipped as she vigorously stirred shortening into her hot-water cornbread. "You backing us up."

Izella sucked her teeth and rolled her eyes before picking up the pace. Her mother never let her forget her lowly place in the house; she even called her Babygal as a constant reminder.

"I'm fixing you girls some turkey necks and hot sauce," announced Evangelist with a wide, drawn smile. "Your favorite since y'all could hold spoons."

"I can't," Ola told her mother with a grimace. "I think I got a bug."

"You stay sick, gal," Evangelist told her firstborn, before grasping a piping-hot cauldron from the potbelly stove with her bare hands and placing it in the middle of their small wooden dining table. "Now, everybody down to your knees for grace."

The three dutifully crouched to their knees in the middle of the spotless kitchen, clasped hands, and closed their eyes for prayer.

Evangelist began. "Oh blessed, kind, loving heavenly Father. Bless this family with the grace of a thousand angels, oh God. Bless this food and the loving hands that prepared it, oh God . . ."

The sisters peeked at each other and giggled. It had

become something of a tradition for them to chuckle during their mother's lengthy prayers. She prayed long, as Ola would say. A food blessing could easily last ten minutes, and by the time it was over, they were starving and their knees ached, but there was no way around it. Their shotgun house was outfitted with oak planked hardwoods. It was small, but it was always clean and filled with strangers, since their tiny living room doubled as a neighborhood church, pastored by Prophetess/Evangelist Flossie Mae Murphy. Everyone from the lowest of the low to the highest of the high was welcome in their small home.

Evangelist had been called to ministry after what she called a young life in the world of sin. Word on the streets said that, before Ola and Izella came along, she had run a successful backyard shot house and bootlegged whiskey and moonshine from Savannah. Even though her mother was a woman of God now, Izella could easily imagine her that way. Evangelist's nature was to bring people in and surround them with joy. When she became a mother, that joy was from the Lord, but as a young woman, she spread that joy through illegal liquor.

"Amen." Evangelist ended her grace. "Now, grab a spoon and fill up before chapel. We've got a full house tonight. That traveling tent revival out of Detroit went up last night. They stop by every year for southern home cooking. Last year was standing room only; remember that, Ola? Babygal was probably too little to remember."

Izella cringed until Ola caught eyes with her and mouthed the word *help*.

"Evangelist?" Izella asked her mother.

"What is it, Babygal?" she replied.

"I forgot to take Mrs. Mac her bread this morning," Izella said with her head hung. "You mind if we miss supper today to walk down to her house?"

Evangelist stopped her stirring to stare at her daughters. "Look here now, girls. I know Mrs. Mac is mean as a snake, but she's been through hell and came out the other side scarred up. It's a wonder she's still walking this side of heaven with all she's been through. I'm not trying to punish y'all. I'm teaching something that can't be taught in school or even at church." Evangelist poked her index finger into Izella's sternum. "Life ain't got a thing to do with what you want. You were put on this earth to help people who can't help themselves. Feed people who can't feed themselves. Even wipe people up when they can't do it, you understand me?"

"Yes, ma'am," said Izella.

"You too?" she asked Ola. "You're the oldest."

"Yes, ma'am," Ola replied. "I understand."

"Now," she said before going back to stirring. "Go on

ahead and take that poor woman what might be her only meal today."

"Yes, ma'am," they said, and scurried out the back door.

"Back before the streetlights!" Evangelist yelled after them.

Ola and Izella quickly walked to the first intersection and turned the corner.

"Thanks," Ola told her sister. "I couldn't stomach one spoonful of turkey-neck juice."

"You're welcome, but you owe me," Izella replied. "I actually wanted them turkey necks. Where we going?" Izella skipped after her big sister.

"Where else?" Ola pointed to the recreation center where her secret boyfriend, Walter, worked.

Izella stopped walking. "Ola, I didn't skip supper to watch you and that boy all hugged up again. Besides, I really do need to take Mrs. Mac her loaf of bread. She crippled and can't walk no more."

"I'll tell you what," Ola started. "You head on over to mean old Mrs. Mac's house, and I'll go hug up with Walter, that way you won't have to see us."

Izella turned back toward home. "I'm telling Evangelist on you."

"Okay, okay, okay." Ola gave in. "I'll go with you to

Mrs. Mac's house, but don't get all into a talk for hours and hours like you do. I don't know why you want me there; she just ignores me. You and Evangelist are the only two folks she likes in the world."

"I'd ignore you, too, if you called me mean old Mrs. Mac," Izella replied. "You don't even try with her. Ask her a question about her life every now and then."

"That's just it. I don't care," Ola said before tugging at one of Izella's fuzzy pigtails.

"Exactly. You're a low-down dirty gal."

Ola stopped cold and folded her arms tightly. "I'm not low-down; I'm just not interested in those old, sad slave stories all the time."

"She hasn't told me one sad slave story, thank you very much."

"Then what y'all talk about in that back room, then?"

"You really don't know?" Izella asked, stunned. When Ola shook her head, she continued, voice hushed. "Mrs. Mac was a reader back in the late eighteens, hiding out in the weeping woods of Savannah. She tells me stories, real stories about curses and hexes and love spells and protections. She can even read my hand and tell what I'm gone be when I get big."

"You lying," Ola said with a phony confidence. She could hardly believe that after months of daily visits to

Mrs. Mac's she had no idea about any of this. "That's a bunch of baloney. What she tell you?"

Izella could tell that Ola was trying to act like she didn't care. "None of your business! You don't even like Mrs. Mac, re-mem-ber?" Izella skipped forward with bigger strides.

"Wait." Ola followed. "You think she can tell me how many babies me and Walter gonna have? Or if we'll have a house with a yard or a fence or a pecan tree?"

"Nope."

"Why?" Ola asked angrily. "I've been bringing her old tail bread every day. She owes me a telling."

"She ain't no fool, Ola. She knows you ain't no friend of hers, and she don't read folks she don't like." Ola tugged at Izella's pigtail again. "Ouch!"

"Make her like me, then."

Izella stopped in front of Mrs. Mac's paint-peeled front fence, pulled the fresh loaf from her satchel, and handed it to her older sister. "Here," she told her before slowly opening the fence. "Do it yourself."

Holding the bread like a newborn baby, Ola slowly walked across the overgrown yard, avoiding busy ant beds and uneven concrete slabs pushed up by unkept tree roots. She'd taken this walk a hundred times before, but now she walked with a new purpose. Her very future depended upon what that old bat told her, and she was about to find out no matter what.

When they reached the rickety front screen, she looked back at her little sister to find her at her heels for support. Though she was younger, Izella was always wiser and more mature than Ola. No one dared speak it, but it was an obvious fact of their sisterhood—the eldest leaned heavily on the youngest.

Sensing Ola's nervousness, Izella called out to Mrs. Mac. "Yooo-hoooo," she hollered before knocking on the screen, which was hanging on by a single hinge.

"Come on in, young'un." A small but significant voice echoed from the heart of the shotgun house.

The sisters snaked their way through the cluttered home. Ola nearly tripped over the sail of a hand-carved wooden ship that was the size of a shoebox. The wood scraped her bare calf, leaving a bloody splinter behind.

"Damn it!" Ola yelled out as blood dripped on wrinkled clothing that was sprawled on the floor. "What the hell was that?"

Ola lifted the bloodstained ship and immediately regretted it. Upon closer inspection, it was no ordinary ship; it was filled with blank-faced enslaved people. She didn't want to see, but she had to look. The tiny details of the carving must've been labored over with the smallest of instruments. A slit-skinny mother held an even thinner baby in her arms; a muscular man crouched with slouched shoulders; a child stood tall and alone. It was a work of horrific art. So beautiful that Ola wanted to cry.

"Put my shit down, gal!" Mrs. Mac's voice broke the spell of the moment.

"How did she know?"

"She's a seer, too," Izella whispered in response. "Blind, broken folks can see better than the rest of us sometimes." Izella eased the ship from her older sister's hand and gently placed it on the cluttered table. "Come on. And don't touch anything."

The sisters headed to the smoke-filled back room, where the distinct smell of marijuana and unfiltered cigarettes was thick and stout. Izella confidently entered the bedroom first and took a seat at the foot of Mrs. Mac's ash-smeared bed.

"You've got worry all over you," Mrs. Mac said in a kind, genuine voice. "What's wrong, child?"

"It ain't me, Mrs. Mac," Izella replied with a small smile. Then she motioned toward the bedroom door, where Ola stood, sneakily plugging her nostrils. "Come on in, Ola. You know Mrs. Mac."

Ola watched her step as she entered the room. Every small stride took strategic avoidance of black ashes, spent tea bags, and little white granules of salt or sand.

"Oh, just walk straight, *you*," Mrs. Mac spat with impatience. Her use of *you* (sounding more like *yew*) as a nickname cut deeper than a cuss—it was a disgusted *you*, a repulsed *you*, a *you* that you'd never want to be called, and both sisters knew it.

"I'm s-sorry," Ola stuttered. "I was just trying to . . . uh. I didn't want to mess up your . . . uh. It's a lot of stuff on your . . . uh."

Izella put her head in her hands as her sister floundered.

"I can't stand folks who don't tell it like they think it. You didn't want to dirty your pretty Mary Janes on this old woman's filthy floor. You as see-through as a crystal siren bell, *you*."

There it was again, that *you*.

"What you want?" Mrs. Mac asked in a repulsed hock. "Spit it."

Ola looked to Izella for help, but Izella was wise enough to keep out of it. Mrs. Mac wasn't the type to be manipulated by youth. She wanted it straight or not at all. Instead of speaking, Izella nodded Ola along like a jockey would a skittish horse.

Ola spoke in a soft voice. "I, ma'am, was hoping to get a read."

Mrs. Mac laughed in a cackle. "You don't need a reader to read you. You one of them gals with boys in your head and not much else. They just want a piece of your new body, and then they want to throw it in the trash. But ain't no point in telling you. You'll know it when it ain't no time left to change it. You won't know you in the trash until the garbageman coming, and then it's too late."

Mrs. Mac paused her contempt to suck a lengthy drag from her cigarette and open her crust-filled eyes, which had been closed the entire time. In her pause, Ola took in the look of the lady. She was half-covered in a dingy bedspread that Evangelist had knitted her a year ago. Her hair looked like it had been cut by a blind person—it probably was, since Mrs. Mac was legally blind. Her skin was layered wrinkles, like a chocolate cake melting in the hot sun, each layer stacking on the one underneath. The whites of her eyes were bloodshot, maybe from the marijuana, and both pupils blue-grayed over like marbles. She was a thrown-away woman. A human being that Ola couldn't imagine living a life worthy of living.

"I hear your judgments in your pretty little head," Mrs. Mac said. "They louder than your words."

Ola knew the old woman had her dead to rights. She had little patience for old women wasting away from hard memories. She hadn't told a soul about it, not even Izella. Ola stood as still as possible. She weighed her next move. She could cut tail and run before the woman had another chance to demean her or read her thoughts. Or she could stand her ground; after all, Mrs. Mac was just a half-blind old woman. What could she possibly do to her? Ola decided on a third option—denial.

"I wasn't thinking anything of the sort, ma'am," she lied. "You have a lovely home, and I'd like very much to hand you your bread so you can enjoy it. Best bread in town, ma'am." Ola placed the loaf on the woman's side table.

Izella again placed her head in her hands and shook it, which Ola took as a bad sign.

"Come here, *you*." Mrs. Mac lifted her unsteady hand. Her hand reminded Ola of the screen door hanging on its hinges. "I'll read you."

Ola walked forward, intentionally ignoring the mess at her feet. She wanted to be read. She wanted to know if her and Walter's picket fence would be white or red. She wanted to find out, once and for all, how many kids they'd have. She wanted to look into her beautiful future and know. She needed to know.

Ola looked at the old woman and smiled; she'd won. She was about to get read.

Mrs. Mac grabbed her hand tighter than Ola thought possible. She cried out in pain, but the old woman wouldn't let go. The pain changed. It started as a simple squeeze, like when the nurse is taking blood pressure, and it turned into a heat like embers. Her hand burned so badly Ola felt tears streaming from the side of her eye. Just as quickly as she'd snatched her hand, the woman let go. It couldn't have been more than a few seconds, but it felt like an hour.

Mrs. Mac stared wide-eyed at the front of Ola's neck. She squinted her blind eyes as if she was focusing in on a small bit of something near Ola's Adam's apple. "Lean in closer," she said.

Ola leaned in a bit.

"Closer than that, *you*."

She leaned in closer still.

Squinting at Ola's neck, Mrs. Mac whispered, almost pitying, "You've got a heartbeat in your neck, gal."

Izella leaped from her seated position and grasped her mouth in horror. But Ola had no idea what that meant. She grabbed her neck, thinking she'd been snake-bitten or rubbed too much into some poison oak. From the look on Izella's face, it had to be bad. "What is it? What does that mean? What's on me?"

"It ain't what's on you," said Mrs. Mac. "It's what's in you. That garbageman already coming for you, child."

•••

Three days after Mrs. Mac dropped her bomb, Ola and Izella were still reeling from the news. Ola was in complete denial, watching her panties day and night, trusting the blood to magically appear. Izella, however, believed the prophecy beyond a shadow of a doubt. She'd seen Mrs. Mac work, and she knew she was the real deal. Mrs. Mac knew things she shouldn't have been able to know. Like how the boys were going to come back from the war twisted in the head. Or how bell-bottoms were going to take over. Hell, she even told Izella that old fuddy-duddy Nixon was gone win the presidency. She also said he'd tuck his tail before his time was up, which turned out to be a whopper, but everybody's wrong sometimes.

Ola was just deciding to go on about her business, with the exception of the hunger strike. Aside from handfuls of aspirin, Ola hadn't eaten a bite since that fateful afternoon, Izella noticed. Ola continued on pressing and folding her bobby socks, hot combing her hair into her favorite Dorothy Dandridge pin curls, and visiting Walter at the rec center like there was nothing growing in her belly. The only evidence of her predicament was the raw egg yolks she kept throwing up. They slept head to foot in the same twin bed, and Izella had a front-row seat to the breaking down of her sister's facade during vomit sessions.

After the last visitor left Bible study, or prayer, or supper, or service, Ola curled her knees into her chest, vomited, and moaned. Low, guttural sounds would come from the depths of her diaphragm. Real pain existed there. Not only the pain of pregnancy, but the pain of denying it. That type of denial took work.

Izella would ease the bobby socks from her sister's feet and massage them until she cried more. Izella knew not to speak or inquire about feelings. That wasn't the Murphy way of doing things; love was a verb in that house. But Izella also knew that Ola needed to cry, and an unprovoked foot rub always did the trick. That night, she noticed the skin of her sister's feet was holding extra fluid. Her pinkie toe looked like a tiny Vienna sausage.

Through her crying, Ola winced at the foot rub.

"Don't squeeze too much." Ola pushed the words through her teeth like they weighed a thousand pounds each. "Can't . . . get . . . no . . . relief."

She didn't have to say it. Izella could look at her usually breezy older sister and see the pain. Izella felt it, too. When Ola moaned, Izella's stomach did a flip. When the tears fell from Ola's almond-shaped eyes, Izella's nose began running. When Ola hurt, Izella did, too. While gently pressing tiny circles into her sister's feet, Izella closed her eyes to silently pray. She started the prayer in her head. It was a prayer that Evangelist would've been proud of, channeling the Holy Spirit with full force and zeal. But the prayer evaporated halfway through, never reaching its amen.

Eyes closed in their small dark bedroom, Izella saw her sister as she had been. Every button fastened, even the one at the very tip-top. No stray hair or lint or wrinkles in her gloves. A sure bet for homecoming queen of the class of 1972. Her head was practically made to wear a crown. And then there was Walter. The blood ran hot in Izella's body when she thought of Walter.

A gentle snore vibrated from Ola so Izella eased her own pillow under her sister's feet, leaving her without one to lie on herself. She fell asleep with her head in her hands.

• • •

The next morning, Izella woke to an unfamiliar sound—throaty and deep with occasional high-pitched tones like a cat with a hair ball stuck. Izella was floating somewhere between being awake and asleep. She couldn't tell if the sounds were happening in real life or in her head. She was angry at the sun shining onto her face so bright that through closed eyes her lids glowed red. She was also angry at her dream, which she couldn't fully remember, but she knew it was about Walter. The sound grew and grew until she couldn't deny that it was real and opened her eyes.

Ola crawled across their bedroom's hardwood floor, the bib of her nightgown covered in the egg-yolk throw up and pee running down her leg. The sound was the sister she loved more than she loved herself. Still, Izella didn't jump to help her. She just watched, frozen.

She watched her sister's crushed pin curls coming undone and crusting with vomit. She watched the remnant drool on the right side of her face. But mostly, she watched the slow creep of her sister's urine. In that moment, Izella knew she'd never be able to forget what she was seeing. She imagined herself, old and gray, waking in the night to see her sister crawling like a kicked stray bitch, making noises she didn't know existed within the human body.

Ola reached for her, hand sticky and foul, but Izella hesitated to take it. Ola noticed the small but significant moment of pause, and it was as if the string that had been holding her up on all fours snipped. Ola fell into a pitiful heap. The string had also held together the two sisters, and in that very moment, they both knew it was severed forever.

That's when Izella leaped from the bed to her sister's side. She'd scrutinize that hesitation for decades, if she lived to see it. Why hadn't she acted quicker? How could she allow her sister to crawl in her own vomit without helping her? And even worse, how could she let her sister see the judgment in her eyes? She'd almost convinced herself that she didn't know the source of that hesitation, but deep down, she knew that it was Ola's weakness she hated. The vomit and pee didn't bother her, not one bit. Most people might find those things disgusting, but to Izella, the defeat was disgusting. Izella made up her mind that she'd never allow herself to fall so far so fast. Not for a boy or a man or a woman or anybody, not ever. If sweet Moses himself set out his staff to lead her out of Egypt, she'd dig a way out her own damn self. No one deserved the power to take down a powerful girl or woman like her sister, she decided. Especially not one as batty as Walter.

"Is it supposed to be like this for every girl?" Izella asked.

Ola didn't answer. She didn't even lift her eyes from the floor. An abject shame clothed her from head to feet.

Izella raked her pin curls loose. "Can you make it to the wash?"

Again, Ola didn't lift her eyes.

"Sister?" Izella asked, beginning to feel the butterflies. "Do I need to get a doctor called?"

Ola forced herself into a sitting position. "Walter," she said. "Get Walter."

Izella felt her nostrils flare, and her blood began to run hot and fast. "I can't stand Walter. He did this to you, and I ain't doing it."

Ola didn't show any emotion at the grandstanding. She simply whispered, "Well I guess I ain't got nobody, then."

Ola and Izella locked eyes as they'd done a thousand times before. Sister to sister. Best friend to best friend. But everything had changed. Loyalties had shifted. Ola's to Walter and Izella's to her single-minded fight for her own future—one she swore wouldn't involve egg-yolk vomit.

"Gals." Evangelist knocked on their bedroom door. "Time for devotion. Come on here."

Izella answered. "We're finishing up cleaning, and fixing up the bed. Be out before you get started."

"Ten minutes and I'm coming back."

"Yes, ma'am," Izella called out, then turned her attention back to her sister. "All right, now you don't worry about this mess. I'll mop it up while you wash that yellow out your hair. And stand up straight or Evangelist will know."

Ola looked at her like a doe would its mama. "What about Walter?"

"You need to be worrying about Evangelist first," Izella said. "Go in there and wash your teeth, too."

Izella lifted Ola to the edge of the bed and propped her like a toddler just learning to sit up. She tiptoed across the hall to get a towel big enough to sop up the yellow and wet another, smaller one to clear the crust from her sister's face. Ola sat there and let Izella wipe her off like a child.

"I need Walter."

"Fine." Izella relented. "I'll get him after devotional. Go get you on some clean panties, now."

• • •

Devotional was quicker than usual. Ironically enough, Evangelist needed to get across town to feed another expecting teenager, named Mississippi, or Missippi for short. Evangelist had found out about Missippi from a mealymouthed church member.

Evangelist was warm toward the baby. She called it "God's" and "little" and "precious" and "innocent." She was, however, much less generous to Missippi, who she unaffectionately referred to as "that ole nasty thang" and "she should've known better" and "was raised better than that."

Izella and Ola always only listened. Even though

Evangelist was technically talking to them, any discussion of sex or pregnancy felt like grown-folks' business that they weren't welcome to comment on. Evangelist had no close friends who weren't parishioners, so the sisters were a dumping ground for her personal woes and angry rants. At times, Evangelist lamented about never having any sisters of her own to talk to and confide in about things. She never missed an opportunity to tell them how blessed they were to have each other, and how so very disappointed she was in her own mother for not providing her at least one sibling.

Izella thought about this often. Analyzed it. Turned it over in her mind, and every day she'd come up with something different. One day, Evangelist had it right and having a sibling was a blessing—instant friendship, someone to talk to, and someone to help warm her freezing bed in the winter. And then on the next day, Izella decided she'd rather be alone in a cold bed than witness her sister's knees knocked out away from underneath her. She usually reached the same conclusion—there would be pros and cons either way, and in the end, everybody wants the thing they don't have, even if they're blessed not to have it.

"Ola, what's the matter with you, child?" Evangelist asked after an especially brutal lashing of Missippi. "You look like hell walking earth."

"You talking about that poor girl all the time," Ola said into her untouched eggs and biscuits. "Girl can't defend herself."

Raw rage filled the kitchen. "What you dare say, gal?" Evangelist said, spitting a mouthful of gravy-soggy biscuit into the air.

Izella jumped to her feet, grabbing hold of the attention. "We need to take Mrs. Mac her loaf. Can we be excused, Evangelist?"

Evangelist gathered the dishes. "I need to get them cheese grits to that hussy Missippi or they'll get all lumped up in the icebox. Poor innocent living in that gal's belly won't take nothing but my cheese grits. Y'all get on to Mrs. Mac's and be back to cook for afternoon prayer." Evangelist paused to glare at Ola, who was still eyeballing her plate. "We're expecting six today. All men, too. They stopping in to be prayed over and eat a good meal on the way over to Tuskegee. Special place in hell for what they did to those men up there. Ola?"

"Yes, Evangelist?" Ola said, trying to insert bass into the two words to make them sound normal, but to Izella, they still sounded sick and abnormal.

"Look at me when I speak to you."

Ola winced, forcing her back straight.

"God don't like ugly one bit, gal," Evangelist said sternly and full of woman-of-the-house wisdom. "Honor your mama. Honor your pastor. And above all things, child, honor Him."

"Yes, ma'am," Ola said dutifully.

"I make up two of those three, you hear?" Evangelist grabbed Ola's chin with such force that she nearly fell back in her chair. "If you test me like that again. In my own goddamn house. I swear I'll smack you. Understand?"

"Yes, ma'am." Jumbo tears fell from Ola's giant eyes. "I understand."

Only then Evangelist released Ola's face and went to wash dishes.

"You're both dismissed," she said. "And Ola! Only the big chicken pieces today for them poor men. Leg quarters, whole breasts. Leave the wings for us, you hear?"

"Yes, Evangelist," Ola said, drained and void of strength.

Evangelist scooped up the container of grits and waved a quick goodbye before stopping herself. She turned around slowly, sending fear through both Izella and Ola. She knew. She'd noticed something. Put two and two together. Now that Izella knew the truth, the signs were so obvious she'd be shocked if Evangelist hadn't figured it out, too. Besides, she'd spent a half hour howling about Missippi's condition, and if she'd just replaced her name with her own daughter's, there you'd have it.

Evangelist's eyes doubled, and she said, "Ola."

"Yes, Evangelist?"

Both sisters were sure. The question was imminent. Three little words: *Are you pregnant?* But instead, she said . . .

"Only the biggest pieces, gal. I mean it. These men have been to hell and back, and their families, too. The least we can do is feed them the best we got."

"Yes, Evangelist."

And as Evangelist left, a breeze of both relief and disappointment blew through the small kitchen. Relief was obvious. Of course they didn't want their mother, the prophetess/evangelist of the neighborhood, to know that ultimate sin slept in the next room. Disappointment, however, was a surprise. They almost wanted her to know. They wanted her to scream and cry and even slap as long as she needed to until she was done, so she could tell them what to do. She was, after all, everyone's adviser. The sisters felt like two baby ducks lost in a mangrove—directionless, knock-kneed, and ripe for picking. The longer Evangelist didn't know, the longer they didn't know what to do. Especially Ola.

Even before the pregnancy, Ola could hardly tie a bow without Izella to pull at one of the strings. Now she was a useless waste of space. The best she could do was build a human inside her body; the rest was up to her little sister, Izella. And whether she judged her or not, they both knew it.

Izella gently placed the back of her hand on her older sister's forehead. "Hot. You gone on back in that bed. I'll get Mrs. Mac her bread and send Walter, too."

Ola perked up as much as a sickling could. "You mind telling him?"

Any other sister might have been surprised, but Izella knew Ola would need her to tell the child's father that he was about to be a father, because she knew her sister. Dread filled up inside her, and the weight sent her into a hunch that a fifteen-year-old girl should never have. "I'll tell him," she said.

As Izella walked out the screen door, she began practicing her speech to the boy she hated. The boy with the shaky hands. The boy who disappeared for months and came back smelling like unwashed hair. The boy who used to be popular and fine, and now parted hallways.

The boy who Izella used to love more than life, and now feared. The boy who got her sister pregnant. The boy who left Georgia wearing cuffed jeans and came back from Vietnam wearing dirty everything.

The boy by the name of Walter.

•••

Izella walked into the recreation center where Walter worked at the basketball check-in. She held back and watched for a few moments. There he stood, in army fatigues, filling and organizing basketballs into perfect lines. He cared too much about the meticulousness of those basketballs. Izella inched toward him like a jungle cat, intuitively cautious not to make any sudden movements.

After he'd returned from the war, no one except Ola wanted to speak to Walter. When Izella, Ola, and Walter were little, he was puffed up like a peacock. But when he came back, he was as deflated as a kicked mutt.

Walter was the first boy Izella knew to drink from the white fountain in front of the white folks. He'd done it on a dare. None of the other children thought he would, but he did. Those white folks called him everything but a child of God that day, but he did it and puffed right along with his chest out. Then all of the other boys formed a line and took a drink to see if the water tasted better.

Even before that, everybody followed Walter's lead. He was a natural at leading, and that's why no one was shocked when he volunteered to go to war at only seventeen. His mama signed his papers one day, and his seat was empty for the next ten months. While he was away, stories about his valor circulated around.

"Walter's taking out that whole fleet by hisself."

"I heard Walter shoot straighter than anybody over there."

"You know Walter gone get that special medal, being brave as he is."

"I think I'll volunteer, too."

Those were the stories. Then when he came home, smelling and shook, nobody was talking about volunteering anymore. Once, in the full lunchroom, he hit the floor at the sound of a freshman girl dropping her tray. It took a call to the principal to get him up. After that, he sat alone. It was as if he wasn't Walter at all anymore. Everybody was scared of or repelled by him. Everyone, that is, except Ola, who seemed to love him more broken than fixed.

"Walter?" Izella asked to see if he was still inside his body or elsewhere.

"You been watching me," he replied, wide-eyed. "Ola okay?" He looked older than he was, but young, too.

Young enough to believe in ghosts and old enough to have actually seen them.

"Not too okay," Izella said, not sure how to tell him his girl was pregnant.

He jumped away from his basketball keep, accidentally leaving the latch undone. Dozens of freshly pumped basketballs fell onto the court. Walter cringed at every bounce, and he almost took off running but stopped himself.

"What's wrong with my girl?" he asked frantically. "I can't lose . . . Where is she now?"

"She at home," she said, pitying. She and her schoolmates were terrified of what had become of Walter in Vietnam. He was proof that the boogeyman existed, and they'd rejected him for it. But not Ola. In that moment, Izella realized that her sister, with all of her naivete, saw Walter deeper than she had. She also realized that he loved Ola more than life itself. "She's going to have a baby, Walter."

Walter sunk into himself.

"Walter?" Izella said, but his eyes were blank. "You all right?"

"I'll . . ." he started. "I ain't right, though. I can't take care of no baby. I ain't right." He locked eyes with Izella. "Tell me what to do."

He grabbed her shoulders too tightly and shook, as if attempting to release the answers from her tiny frame. Pain shot through Izella's upper body. He was strong, wild, almost rabid. Izella decided to take it—the pain, the fear, the haphazardness of the basketballs, and Walter and Ola, all of it.

Izella. The youngest of Evangelist's girls. Fifteen years old. Hadn't even gotten her period yet was again being asked to solve the problems of her elders. Everyone thought her capable, even Evangelist. Even though she wouldn't let her cut the vegetables, she occasionally asked her for advice about her parishioners. She'd never once asked Ola.

The truth was Izella didn't know what to do. Ola was expecting, Walter lost his mind in the jungle somewhere, and Evangelist was too busy saving the world one meal at a time to notice any of it. There was no one to turn to except Izella. She had to step up. She had to be the strong one. Her stomach was turning from the pressure, but she had no choice. She was the only one left with good sense. She stood there, firm in Walter's uncontrolled grasp, equally flattered and petrified. She forced her chin up.

"You go to my house and sit with Ola," Izella told Walter with the authority of a parent. "She's probably sick at her stomach, needing somebody to clean her up and rub her back. I'll figure out what to do about the other."

"What are you going to do?" Walter asked, eyes still wild.

"Just go on now."

Walter dutifully went on, dodging basketballs like land mines. As he turned the corner, leaving the gymnasium, Izella let herself shrink into a fifteen-year-old. While speaking to Walter, she'd been projecting herself into something older. More mature. Something with a full life of wisdom behind her. But when there was just her left, standing in the middle of the basketball court, surrounded by loose balls, she broke. No crying, never that. Izella broke in Izella's way—the thinking way. She allowed her thoughts to disorganize and jumble into one another. She shook her head as they made the rounds through her mind like shooting stars.

Ola's pregnant. Oh God. Evangelist will send her away. Would she really send her away? Of course she would. She called Missippi a hussy all day long and turned her nose up to her. Sent away was probably the best thing for that child. Ola can birth it, come back, and put on her bobby socks like nothing had happened. But Izella knew that wasn't her sister. Ola would want that baby. So, what if Evangelist let her raise it? She'd have to marry. Make the thing legal in front of God and the congregation. Ola, a wife. To Walter. Poor Walter. Shook Walter. Walter can't hardly take care of his own self. The old Walter would've raised a good baby. A strong baby with a straight backbone for what's what, but this new Walter needed quiet. New babies don't know quiet. Even he knows he ain't right no more.

A baby can't be brought into a world as messed up as this one here, Izella thought. She hadn't known many babies in her lifetime. Hadn't even changed a diaper that she could recall, but she knew that a baby would suffer being brought up by Ola. She was too young and dumb to be a mama. Ola dreamed in the daytime about pretty dresses and hair bows. She still avoided the cracks in the sidewalk for the chance it might break Evangelist's back—she wouldn't admit to it, but Izella knew it. What kind of mother could she make? A mama that drops a baby on its head, that's what kind.

Izella shook her thoughts away again, trying to reorganize herself into the sister with the right answer. Best thing for everybody is no baby. No baby for Evangelist to know about, no baby to send Walter into the shakes, no baby to split Ola from a girl into a mama. No baby. But how could a growing baby in a belly turn into no baby in a belly?

Izella lifted the loaf of bread from her deep pocket. Mrs. Mac. She'll know what to do. She fled the gym and nearly squeezed the loaf into a thousand crumbles.

• • •

On her way to Mrs. Mac's house, Izella tidied up her mind. The answer was clear and obvious—baby needed to become no baby.

When Izella turned onto Mrs. Mac's block, she saw her sitting on her porch swing. The creaking sound echoed through the neighborhood. The high squeak gave Izella pause and stopped her in her tracks. Slow, lengthy whines emitted from the rickety chains that were barely holding Mrs. Mac's small body. They were louder than they should've been, and they packed more of a punch. The sound of a porch swing was a typical thing in her neighborhood, a welcome thing. It usually reminded Izella of fresh-squeezed lemonade with ice and seeds floating inside, but this felt like warning sirens going off.

Izella slowly opened the gate to Mrs. Mac's yard and closed it behind her. "How did you manage to get outside, Mrs. Mac?"

Mrs. Mac looked like a different woman than she had the day before. Hair combed, teeth washed, and day dress clean, she looked healthy and strong for her age. Izella noticed a new glow in her red-boned skin. She looked like she'd greased herself with one of the butters—shea or cocoa.

"I ain't felt this good in a minute, child," Mrs. Mac said with a tinge of chipper. "Where your sister?"

Mrs. Mac had all ten of her fingers clasped together into a pulsing bulge. She was giddy with the knowing, and her anticipation was as thick as fresh-cut bacon. Izella felt herself standing at a fork in her life. One way was right, and one wasn't, but neither were ideal, and she couldn't decide which was which. Izella should've dropped the crumpled bread at Mrs. Mac's feet and run off. She should've made something up—another well visit, or a grocery store necessity, or something. But she didn't.

"We need this baby gone, Mrs. Mac," Izella said, forcing every word out of her mouth individually, pretending they didn't make up the single most important sentence she'd ever said in her life. "Can you help us get rid of it?"

Mrs. Mac's skin shone even more alive. "Last night," she said with a wide smile, revealing very old teeth, "I dreamed you was coming here to ask me that there question, child. When a knowing woman dreams something like that, it means death is a long way off. It means death is gone let me see this whole thing play out till the ending of it. I got a lot of life ahead of me, child, thanks to you and your sister. You two keeping me on this side a little while longer, and for that reason, I'm gone help you get rid of that old baby."

Izella exhaled a sigh of resolution. She hated unfinished things. Izella was the type to sit for hours lifting stuck gum off the walkway. The type to read an awful book all the way until the end. Right or wrong, Mrs. Mac had given her an ending, and that fact had let a little anxious air out of her.

•••

Izella ran home feeling a little lighter. She turned left on Westcliff, just like every other day. She found herself avoiding the cracks, just like Ola. She'd never done that before. Not once. In an instant, she decided to cut through Mrs. Stoke's pecan-shell-littered backyard and jump Mr. Turner's fence, careful to avoid kicking over his fermenting white-lightning jugs near the back shed.

Izella never used the shortcut when she and Ola walked home together. Ola was edgy as a shot cat about people. Always avoiding the off chance that she might run into another soul as much as possible. A popular recluse, Ola relied heavily on her beauty. Outside their small bedroom, she showed little of her personality, not even to Evangelist. Lively and easy with Izella, but buttoned up and stuffy with most everybody else. The only other somebody Ola could be free with was Walter.

And there he was, pacing rings around her backyard.

Shaking his head back and forth and up and down and back and forth and up and up and up and screaming at the clear blue sky with a long, drawn-out "Whyyy?" Meanwhile, Ola hunched over the back porch, spitting up the faint yellow slime that comes at the tail end of the egg yolks.

The lightness left Izella, and her legs refused to propel her body forward from Mr. Turner's yard. Shielded by thick, unpruned rose and raspberry bushes, Izella stood motionless as if shot by a stun gun. The blue sky began to change, and all of a sudden, she smelled it. Fresh rain mixed with 100 proof.

"Stripe of that on your tongue will make you forget about all that madness 'cross the way, young'un," drawled Mr. Turner. He motioned a gallon glass jug of clear liquor toward her. "Gone on, chile. I ain't seen somebody needing a capful of lightning much as you in a while."

"What I look like to you?" Izella snapped before she realized. "A fool? You sweating rotgut from your pores."

She jumped the fence as Mr. Turner called her a little bitch.

"Walter," Izella urged, quickly approaching. "Come inside before the whole neighborhood sees you yelling at the empty sky. Drunk old Mr. Turner already saw you. Grab up Ola and bring her to the bed."

Izella went ahead of them to check the bedroom. Just as she'd suspected, it was a wreck. She busied herself in a frenzy of cleaning. Stripping their yellow-crusted bed and throwing a clean cover overtop as Walter guided her wriggling sister on top of it.

Izella stared directly into Walter's face to calm his wild eyes. "I need you to wipe her up, you hear?" She nodded to encourage him to nod back, and then he did. "After she's good and clean, take that brush and pick the throw up out her hair, you hear?" When he nodded along, she continued. "After that, put her in the blue-and-white paisley-print dress with fresh bobby socks from that top drawer."

Walter raised his hand like he was in school. "What's paisley mean?" he asked.

Izella shook her head and softened her tone, forcing patience into herself. "The only blue-and-white dress in the closet. Now, I'm going to clean up the yellow in the bathroom so Evangelist don't see. I ain't got but a hour before she gets back home. Can you do all that for me?"

When Walter nodded again, Izella went to work cleaning up Ola's mess. Like always.

• • •

"This house smell like Pine-Sol!" Evangelist yelled through the cracked door with glee. "You a child of God, Babygal."

She grabbed her youngest into a bear hug and hurried to the kitchen.

"Thanks, Mama," said exhausted Izella.

Evangelist reappeared in the doorway, the glee replaced by furrowed, concerned brows. "What's wrong?" She must know the truth about everything.

Izella glanced down at her cleaning shirt to see if Ola's pregnancy was written out in big, bold letters. She felt her pockets for something to give away the whole truth. She found nothing. "What you mean?" Izella finally asked, confused and uncomfortable.

"You never call me mama, Babygal, unless something's real wrong," Evangelist said before taking a seat in front of her. "Sit a minute."

"Nothing's wrong, Ma . . . I mean, Evangelist." Izella shook her head at her own fluster and sat next to her mother. "I'm fine . . . I really am . . ."

"You don't look fine." Evangelist redirected Izella to sit on the floor between her knees. "How 'bout I work some of these knots out your head and you tell me what's what."

Izella knew better than to tell her no. Between parishioners coming and going and Ola's tantrums, alone time with her mother was a rare privilege in their home. And Izella, mature as she was, always longed for alone time with her busy mother. She wasn't about to turn that down. Pregnant sister or not.

"Tell me about it, Babygal."

As the wide-toothed comb dug into her scalp, Izella let the tension go from her face and hands and lower back. Evangelist applied just the right amount of comb pressure to make it almost hurt, but not quite. Izella's eyes rolled back a bit when her mother found a patch of dandruff and went to scratching it up. Large flakes flew and floated into her lap until her dark cleaning shorts looked whitish.

"You got a lot of good growing dandruff, Babygal," Evangelist said. "But you ain't said what's troubling you yet."

Izella wanted to blurt it out. It was the perfect time and place. In their calm, tiny, empty living room at Georgia dusk. Remnants of a hard rain dinging the roof and crickets screaming their white noise. Pine-Sol-soaked air and love. Pure love from a mama, filling up the shot-gun house.

Just say it, she thought. You need help figuring this out. No fifteen-year-old should have a say in such things. Don't know enough to have a say. Tell your mama the truth, or you'll regret it. It would take less than a few seconds to say it out loud. And besides, you didn't do anything wrong. This is all Ola's doing. Stupid, stupid Ola did this to herself. Why should you have to beat yourself to death trying to decide what stupid girls who go out and get pregnant by war-broke boys do with their babies? You ain't even been kissed. What do you know? Not a damn thing, that's what. Tell your mama. Izella opened her mouth to speak.

"All right then," Evangelist started. "I'll tell you 'bout my day, and then you might feel like telling after. I took Missippi grits this morning. She's growing like a stuffed hog, that one. Child can barely fit through the doorway to grab her grits. I feel like that baby gone wind up raised in a house of hell with all kind of sin and debauchery. And she flighty, too. Clueless gal don't know her head from a hole in the wall. Ain't got a bit of business having no young'un. Big as she is, I wonder if she having twins, Lord have mercy. I thank heaven every day I ain't got to worry about that kind in my house. I work every day to make sure that ain't what my girls are doing. I tell you what I know. That's what you get when you ain't got God in your home. Spare the rod, spoil the child, and that daddy ain't never home with that poor child to give her no real discipline. And the mama been dead . . ."

Izella zoned out after that. Evangelist could go on bashing Missippi for a full hour without breathing. Her mother accepted all sin as forgivable except out-of-wedlock pregnancy. Izella had seen her forgive adulterous deacons, sloppy alcoholics, even murderers, but a young girl having a baby for a boy who didn't want her was the ultimate sin.

And here she was with one of those girls in her own back room. If she knew, she'd die. She'd have a heart attack right there in the living room and die. Izella didn't want her mama to die. She loved her mama just as much as she loved her sister. She couldn't tell her, because she couldn't kill her.

"Where's your sister at?" Evangelist asked after the longer-than-usual Missipi rant.

"She sleep."

"That child can sleep clear through a twister in her front yard," Evangelist said with a small laugh. "Now sweep up this dandruff. We got to cook for the Tuskegee boys. They deserve the best we can give—chicken thighs, potatoes mashed up, and I bought a big bag of rutabagas from the farmer. You feel up to fixing them? You make rutabagas better than grown women."

Any other day, Izella would've been honored. In their house, that type of responsibility meant high esteem. It meant that her mother had faith in her. Izella longed for a day that simple. But those days were gone for now, maybe forever.

"I'll fix them up," Izella replied.

"Good gal. And wake up your sister so she can help you cut. Don't let her season them, though. 'Cause Lord have mercy."

• • •

All six men wore hats and overalls. To Izella, they looked like elderly brothers—all sunburned, with thinning hair and short breath. Normal men like any other swinging by for supper. If Izella hadn't known the truth, she would've thought them regular parishioners.

Evangelist kept referring to them as "them poor men." So Izella expected them to be pitiful. They were not pitiful. They were comical and full of life and stories. Izella's favorite smiled wider than a river. His beard had long gone gray and his eyes, too. Mr. Melvin was his name.

"How old you?" he asked Izella as she introduced herself. When she replied, he flew off into a story about his fifteenth birthday in Macon County, Alabama. "Sit down, boys, and I'll tell y'all 'bout it."

The other five men led him to Evangelist's favorite rocking chair in the back corner of the living room as if he was their ringleader. Slow, gray, old, and more full of life than all the people put together under that roof.

"Careful, madam," he started as the five left his side.

"I might have to take this here chair right along home with me when I leave."

Evangelist laughed in a way she rarely laughed—full bellied and with pure, untouched joy. Ola, however, stood stiff and barely visible, half-hidden behind the long living room curtains.

"Go fix these nice men big plates, gals," Evangelist instructed her daughters.

"Madam," said Mr. Melvin. "Can I hold on to the fifteen-year-old for a quick bit? I promised her a story, and I hate to tell a lie. Even a little one. I promise to be quick."

The other five men laughed at the last statement.

"When he says quick, ma'am," said the youngest-looking man, in khaki corduroy overalls, "he don't never mean quick."

Mr. Melvin waved him off. "Don't listen. They just jealous of my wit. God didn't make but one of me, ma'am."

The rest of them couldn't help but nod in agreement.

"He's right on that."

"He ain't never lying."

"Mm-hmm."

Evangelist smiled. "Yes, sir, Mr. Melvin. Me and my oldest can handle fixing y'all up something to eat. And please, call me Flossie."

Ola and Izella reflexively caught eyes and smiled. It was the first smile Izella had seen out of her sister in days. It was fast and beautiful and full of that magnetic connection they'd had since her birth. They hadn't heard their mother ask anyone to call her anything but Evangelist ever. It was a first, right there in that living room. Even the sisters would never have known their mother's first name if not for the mail. And there she was, asking the charming gray man to call her that—Flossie. Definitely a first.

The evening was sweet and simple. And by the end, even Ola joined the circle of laughter. Izella drank it up like sweet tea. Her family as it used to be. As it should always be. Feeding those who started the night as strangers and would leave as brothers and sisters and mothers and fathers in Christ. Ministering through home cooking and kindness and no judgment whatsoever. Following the lead of those in need. Above all, laughter.

Mr. Melvin lifted a hidden cloud from overtop the small house with his Macon County stories. With the exuberance of a child, he told about sharecropping in hundred-degree weather, and the Tuskegee Airmen, and, finally, his bad-blood disease, syphilis.

He spoke about it as if he were speaking about someone else's unfortunate situation. Izella hadn't expected him to speak of it. Most older men she knew puffed themselves up, but never revealed their struggles out loud. She'd always been bugged by that—men being big and bad and strong, but never human. Mr. Melvin, however, showed himself to the world unfiltered, flaws and all. He was the best man she'd ever met.

"The bad blood was a lie—y'all know that much," he said with a small grin that never completely left his face. "They shot us up with poison, and Lord help us, we was being led to slaughter like baying sheep."

"Are you angry at the white folks for doing that to you?" Izella asked. Her mother slung daggers at her through her eyeballs. "Sorry."

"She's lost her manners," Evangelist told Mr. Melvin. "Know better than to ask grown folks questions like that, child."

"Pardon, Ms. Flossie," Mr. Melvin said before laying his large hand overtop hers and winking at her. "It's value in an inquisitive child. And, by goodness, it's a good question. If I may, I'd like to answer it. With your permission, of course."

"Of course." Evangelist softened like left-out butter. "My home is your home, kind sir."

"Angry I am, child." Mr. Melvin turned his wise eyes onto Izella. "Angry for my mama's mama who was brought over here in a big boat with no choice in the matter. Angry for my mama who picked cotton and nursed babies that wasn't hers. Angry for my daddy who sharecropped for thieving men. Angry for *your* mama who works her body and brain and hands bare with little recognition outside of her living room. Angry for these five men here with me who have to deal with my long-winded tongue." He chuckled. "Angry for they wives having to deal with the bad blood, too. And for they children for having to dodge it. Also, child, I'm angry for you." He stared at Izella, or through her. "And you." He then rested his gaze on Ola, who became noticeably uncomfortable.

"Why us?" Izella asked before she realized it. "Sorry, I . . ."

"It's okay, Babygal," Evangelist said in an uncharacteristically sweet tone; she *really* liked this man.

"Come here." Mr. Melvin motioned Izella and Ola to stand in front of him. "I got something to tell y'all."

Izella and Ola slowly made their way to his chair.

"Look here, both of you," he told them. "Times are getting better. But it's slow as a drip carving out a crater in rock. My mama's mama was a drip. My mama was a drip. I'm a drip. Your mama is a drip. And you both drips, too. Drip, drip, drip, drip. All of us. Slow, steady, making a tunnel to break the dam of real freedom.

"One time, when I was a boy, younger than both of you, I held a penny in my hands and flipped it high up in the air. It stayed up so long that I sat cross-legged there in the dirt, and waited all afternoon for it to come back down to me. The sun was so bright, I had to look away from it. I tapped my bare feet, drew faces in the ground, held my breath, turned circles, and spun and spun and spun. When the penny finally came back down, it had lost its copper color and was all dented up and battered. It came back different, but more valuable. Not more valuable to any other man in the world, though, you see?

"If I walk in a store and slide that penny over the counter, any old man will just see a beat-up penny that's lost its copper. He'll see a penny that's been clear to hell and back and came out not worth nothing but a single cent. But I see something different. I see me—an old, strong, resilient, powerful thing that may not be worth much of nothing to the world, but to God, I'm worth everything.

"I swear that thing flipped up so high it touched heaven, God kissed it, and sent it back to me." Mr. Melvin lifted the penny from his pocket and handed it to Ola. "I only got one. I wish I could split it right down the seam for y'all gals, but I can't. You keep this for me. I feel like it's done just about all it can do for me."

The entire room was in tears. Everyone, that is, except for Izella.

Izella never cried. It wasn't her way.

• • •

The next day, Walter held Ola as they walked up Mrs. Mac's cracking pathway. Izella followed closely as an extra precaution in case Ola fell backward.

Ola was in bad shape. She'd moaned throughout the night, and Evangelist nearly beat the door down at midnight. Izella had to lie about stumping her toe on the bed frame to get her to go away. Walter wouldn't leave Ola's window. He stood beside the crack, whispering sweet encouragements to Ola all night. Through her moans, she begged him to go home and get some rest, but he refused.

Mrs. Mac burst through the screen door like a teenager. It was as if she were growing younger every day. Three days before, she had been a bedridden woman on the verge of death, but now she looked like a fifty-year-old. And a good fifty with shiny, silvery-gray, shoulder-length hair, glowing brown skin, and a springy, purposeful step. She'd been reborn through Izella and Ola's agony.

"Come on in, chillun!" she said, revealing a mouth filled with aged, sturdy teeth. "I got y'all ready some ginger-root tea made."

Izella went in first. The house had been rearranged completely, and despite the dust, it was relatively clean. A solid green-velvet settee with wooden claw-feet had been flipped right side up, the oak coffee table glistened, and the thick fibers of the purple area rug were still a hodgepodge from a brisk broom sweep. But the dramatic focal point of the room was the curio. The day before it was covered with a large, dirty sheet. It was out now. Magnificent and terrifying. Candlelit mahogany, tempered glass, as tall as the ceiling, and as wide as the full back wall, it dominated the small room. The curio itself was beautiful in a priceless sort of way, but the insides made it startling.

Men.

Every glass square held a hand-carved man. They looked to be made of acrylic and driftwood and sawdust and red dirt. Their eyes mismatched buttons snatched from random garments. Some had pipes hanging from their mouths, and others had no mouths, only shut zippers. One especially disturbing figure boasted a real train conductor's hat—it looked to be the only item in the curio that wasn't carved or molded. Izella counted forty-nine men—seven rows by seven columns. She had always been good at her multiplication tables. There was one empty slot at the very top. The fiftieth.

Ola's loud moans snapped Izella back.

"Ahhhh." Ola yelled out a guttural, deep sob.

It sounded very much like a constipated bowel movement multiplied by a million, Izella thought. She sprang to her sister's side. Walter looked so shaky and terrified that she feared he'd let her drop.

Izella caught Mrs. Mac smiling at her sister's despair, and the instinct to run shot through her body.

"Sit her down here, child." Mrs. Mac motioned toward the circular dining table with four cushy chairs, as if expecting them. "The gravid one next to me."

Mrs. Mac had already placed piping-hot ginger tea at each place setting. The smell was sharp, like needles to the nostrils.

"Sip it slow," Mrs. Mac told Ola. "The root will unruffle that babe." Without permission, she lifted Ola's sweat-filled shirt, placed her hand on her lower stomach, and closed her eyes. "It's no wonder you screaming, child. She a jumping jack in there, twirling and leaping like a hopscotch."

"She?" Ola said, perking up. "I'm having a little girl?"

"Sip," said Mrs. Mac before lifting the cup to Ola's bottom lip. "Better?"

Ola lifted her chin to force a swallow; then she smiled. "Better."

"That root tells them old babies to quit their jig," she

said, satisfied. "And yes, this is as girly a girl as I seen in a minute, child."

A tear squeezed from the corner of Ola's eye, and she looked at Walter. "A baby girl," she told him.

He didn't smile or cry or anything; he just shook his head in silence.

They ain't no parents, Izella thought. They barely teenagers. The both of them.

"How do we get rid of it?" Izella interjected.

"You shut your filthy mouth!" Ola spat. "Ain't no getting rid of nothing happening here. I'm having a girl, you hear?"

"Where you gone raise up this girl you gone have?" Izella asked angrily. "Evangelist's house? Where she gone sleep? At the foot of our twin bed? Get real, you stupid girl! Your head is lost in the clouds."

Ola couldn't think of anything to say. Her hurt was too overwhelming to steer through by herself, so she looked to Walter. He was still shaking his head and rocking back and forth, arms folded tightly. They were a mess of their own making.

Mrs. Mac reached for Ola's hand. "You ain't got no place to put no baby, child. You ain't even got no place to put yourself."

Ola wailed. Not in physical pain—it was a bottomless, indescribable pain. A realization that she was the only somebody in the world who wanted her baby girl to breathe the free air. Even more than that, a realization that everyone around the table was right. Walter was a broken boy, and she had nothing in the world that belonged only to her—even her tiny bed was half Izella's. They couldn't possibly raise a baby. She searched her mind for someone to blame. Walter was too frail. Mrs. Mac was too foreign. Evangelist was too blind. Izella was left.

"I'll never forgive you for this." She locked eyes onto her sister like an eagle to prey, and then turned her gaze to Mrs. Mac. "Go on, then—take my baby girl back to heaven, where she belongs."

Mrs. Mac smiled, rubbing friction between her palms. "What are we waiting for, then?" Mrs. Mac pulled a crisp white sheet from a water basin in the center of the table and poured a beef-talla-smelling hot liquid from a heavy steel pitcher. Then she uncovered a small red bowl of cluck and guts, squeezed them with her fingers, and dropped them, too, into the basin. Finally, she lifted a bar of lye soap from her deep, sewn-on pocket and worked the slop into a lather. "All right, kids. This baby needs to be thrown into the wash."

MISSIPPI

21 Weeks

Missippi craved Evangelist's cheese grits. She waited in her room for them to arrive every day, pining for them from even before her belly started to grow. They were all she had left to look forward to. Her paper dolls cut from Papa's old newspapers and marble set only kept her attention for so long. She was fourteen now. Too old for all that baby stuff anyway.

She'd read from Genesis to Revelation more than twice. It was the only book she was allowed to own, but sometimes she couldn't understand it. Most of the Old

Testament just felt like big chunks of words and strange names strung together, making up nonsense. Only Proverbs made real-life sense to her. She didn't dare tell her papa that.

She hadn't told him about the half-buried copy of *The Bluest Eye* she'd found peeking from the trash heap at the rec center, either. What were the odds of Missippi showing up at the center that day to pull that particular book out the dump? Destiny sent Pecola to keep her company. A few of the middle pages were torn out, but Missippi used her imagination to fill in the blanks. Destiny also did that, since Missippi had a wonderful imagination. She loved Pecola and Claudia and Frieda. Laughed right along with them and cried with them, too. But Papa would never approve of that book. To Papa, it was the Bible, or nothing.

He was a good papa, but he stayed gone more than a mama would have, and Missippi's mama had died long before she was old enough to know what was what. Missippi fantasized about having a mama every minute of every day. She'd daydream about greasing each other's scalps with Vaseline, playing paper dolls, and cooking cheese grits like Evangelist and her two girls did. And maybe even reading together. Something other than the Bible, though.

Missippi was a girl without a mama, and for that reason, there were many things she didn't understand about being a girl. When she'd first got her period, she thought she was dying. She took her soiled panties to her papa. He exchanged them for a quarter and sent her on her way, but he didn't tell her where to go or what to buy. The following morning, he had to leave for a long haul to South Carolina. She'd spent the quarter on sweets and stuffed paper towels inside herself until a teacher showed her a sticky pad to put on her underpants.

Missippi wore too-big clothes and knew how to hoe a backyard with her own two hands. She could fix a transmission without a guidebook and change all four tires in less than ten minutes, but she couldn't fix her rat's-nest hair to save her own life. Missippi was a girl without a mama, and it showed.

She heard a knock on the door. "Hello?" asked Evangelist. "I got your grits, Miss Missippi."

Missippi jumped from her bed and nearly slid across her bedroom floor to get to those grits. She opened the door to Evangelist. "Thank you for coming. I've been looking forward to seeing you."

"It's hot," Evangelist said before handing over the colorful, crochet-covered pot. "I'll pick up the pot from you tomorrow."

"Leaving so soon?" Missippi asked, obviously disappointed. "Stay a minute. Papa's out a few days. Haven't spoken to anyone in a while."

"I got company coming to town later on, Miss Missippi," Evangelist said, irritated by her longing. "Cooking and cleaning don't get done all on its own, now."

"Yes, ma'am," said Missippi, intentionally showing distress in her eyes. She was anxious to talk to someone, especially a woman. "I'll just talk to my paper dolls, then."

"Fine." Evangelist shoved past her and made her way to the kitchen. "May as well fix something up for dinner while I'm here. What y'all got to cook in here?"

Evangelist wasn't the type to just sit on a couch and discuss the weather. She needed to move her busy hands.

"Miss Missippi," Evangelist said like any mother would say the name of a daughter in big trouble. "Ain't no excuse for this wrecked kitchen. Come on here, baby in your belly or no baby in your belly. Young girl's kitchen is supposed to be her heaven. If it ain't clean and smelling like Pine-Sol, she ain't got no business calling herself a girl."

Missippi hung her head for real this time. It was the first time a woman had shared that bit of wisdom with her. A steadfast, workable snippet to transform Missippi from an engine-grease-covered tomboy into a girl. She decided to hold on tight to it. Clench it into her memory.

Clean your kitchen and you're a girl. I'll be doggoned, she thought.

"Do your girls do it, too?" Missippi asked, wanting desperately to be more like Izella and Ola. Peeking through her dingy, dust-covered blinds, she'd been watching them for years. Walking the sidewalks together. Mimicking Ola's skipping and avoiding cracks in the walkways. Spinning around and around her living room like Izella did sometimes. She'd even asked her papa for bobby socks to be more like them, but he'd given her a firm no and sent her to her room. He was a good papa. But he wasn't a mama. Not even close.

Missippi had never spoken to them, but Izella was her favorite. She was less buttoned up than her sister, freer. More likely to wave at folks sitting on the porches and less likely to have straight hair parts. Ola, though, never dared leave her house with a crooked hair part or a wrinkled skirt. She belonged on the cover of *Jet* magazine, the way she put herself together. But she didn't seem to like nobody other than her sister. The hundreds of times Missippi had seen Ola walk up and down the street, she'd never witnessed her share a genuine smile with a stranger. And Missippi wasn't the only somebody to notice. She'd seen other kids shoot dirty looks at Ola behind her back. Looks that said, *Who she think she is?* loud and clear without saying it in words. But to Missippi, Ola's attitude never came off as snobbish; it looked shy, reserved, even scared of people on the outside. Actually, on second thought, Ola was her favorite.

"My girls been cleaning long as they been walking," Evangelist said with the utmost pride. "They keep house. One day, when they marry, they gone keep house better than any other woman would know how to."

Missippi watched Evangelist beam at the thought of her girls marrying and cleaning up. She remained silent and watched Evangelist spill Pine-Sol into pools on the counters and floors. Still smiling, Evangelist continued on. "No man, especially no Southern man, wants a woman to keep a nasty house. I'm training my two. They know how to wipe up, cook, dust, sweep, scrub. And not just they houses, but they bodies, too. A clean temple is as important as a clean house. No good reason left to buy a cow when he can get the milk for free."

Missippi watched and thought. Wipe up, cook, dust, sweep, scrub, wipe up, cook, dust, sweep, scrub, wipe up, cook, sweep, dust, scrub, milk for free . . .

"You mean," Missippi inquired, "milk for free to boys?"

Evangelist pushed herself from the floor, where she'd been obsessively scrubbing at a pool of Pine-Sol. "A girl's body is her temple, Miss Missippi," she said, looking her in the eye, woman to woman. "Boys ain't got no business tracking they dirty shoes through your temple. They roll in the dirt. Sweat the salt of devilish lust. They dogs, Miss Missippi. Dogs tear down a girl's temple till ain't nothing left but bare bones and sticks."

Missippi caught sight of her hands—smeared black from engine grease. Her nails filthy from digging up vegetables without gloves.

"I can clean up, Evangelist," she said, feeling desperation creeping in. "Wipe up, cook, dust, sweep, scrub, dust . . . Or is it dust and then scrub? I can do it. I can do everything you say. And I love to read, too, quiet as it's kept! If I could, I'd have a whole house of books. Boys like smart girls as much as they like clean girls, don't they? I'm smart and I can fix things and I'm a quick study. I can be just as good as your two if you show me how." The pity in Evangelist's gaze was so thick Missippi could cut it with a butter knife. "You looking at me like I'm not worth nothing, ma'am."

"Naw, Missippi," Evangelist said before reaching for her tangled nest of hair. "God says you worth gold. Who am I to say different? But I ain't gone stand in your kitchen and tell you no lie. Ain't no man gone touch you after you done went out and did that," she said, motioning to Missippi's stirring stomach.

Missippi couldn't think of anything to say in response to such meanness. She watched as Evangelist squatted back to the floor to edge away at the poured Pine-Sol like she hadn't just ruined Missippi's hopes for a better life. Missippi wondered if all mamas spoke about things they didn't understand like this mama just had. If mamas made these types of guesses without bothering to ask any questions. If they were all so dumb and cruel and mean and stupid. If so, she thought, she didn't want one no more.

• • •

The following morning, Missippi stood in her tiny checkerboard kitchen, stunned. Evangelist had left the house smelling of pure Pine-Sol. Every dish cleared of the stubborn spots that only the strongest fingernail could scratch away. Every burner on the stove was free of seared-on crumbs and grease. And every pot gleamed, with the exception of the one filled to the brim with grits.

Missippi couldn't figure how she'd done it in less than two hours. Evangelist was a single-minded cooking, cleaning, evangelizing machine. Missippi wanted to be impressed and thankful, but all she was was hurt. Evangelist, with all of her do-gooder tendencies, threw daggers at girls who didn't deserve them. She'd taken one outside look at Missippi and judged. And judge not, lest ye be judged, so says the Lord. Someone who called herself Prophetess Evangelist should know this better than anyone.

Missippi wanted a mama more than any diamond, but she'd never considered the possibility that having a mama might be worse than not having a mama. She'd never thought that a mama could look into a girl and draw out hurt, maybe just for the sake of hurting. It depended on the mama, Missippi guessed.

She heard a knock on the door and assumed Evangelist had left something behind. No one ever came knocking on her door without a good solid invite from her papa. He was a good papa.

Missippi tiptoed to the living room curtains to peek out. Her papa told her never to do that. He said it was tacky and made her look like she didn't have home training, although he never wanted her to answer the door. In a perfect world, Papa wanted Missippi to curl up real quiet and wait for whoever had the nerve to come by unannounced to leave, but Missippi was entirely too lonely for that level of restraint. She was cooped-up and curious as a cat.

"Coming!" she said in a chipper voice. "Don't go nowhere! I'm coming!"

She heard a man clear his throat. She paused. It was early afternoon. Probably the mailman with a special package or the milkman or the iceman or maybe it was a lost traveler just looking for a little something to eat. Grits on the stove, she thought. More than enough to share with a weary wanderer.

Maybe he was a powerful man. Not too old, early twenties, just out of school, ready to settle down with a pretty young girl who knows how to dig in the dirt, change a quick tire, and tell a made-up tale of Pecola and the lost middle pages of *The Bluest Eye*. Or maybe it was a war-weary grunt to take her out of her Pine-Sol-smelling, lonely house, where only a judgmental Evangelist came by every day. She'd show her, Missippi thought. She'd spoken all of that "no man gone touch you" mess over her like her future was set. But a good, strong man at the door would be a sound win for her.

She made a quick pit stop by the bathroom to scrub the dirt from her palms and break off a comb in her grease-stuck hair. Then she hid *The Bluest Eye*, because what if he didn't like smart girls at all? She continued trying to finger the broken comb's teeth from the roots of her thick hair.

"Coming!"

She decided to give up before her miracle left the porch. Skipping toward the heavy wooden door, she visualized a better life. Just like a princess stuck away in a tower, she was. Waiting. Dreaming—awake and sleep. He was finally here.

The door creaked open, and there he was.

An inaudible air left her body. She dropped her head in automatic submissiveness to him. She felt like a kicked dog.

"Hey, sweet thang," he said before blowing his sour breath into her ear.

He smelled horrible—half like a dying thing and half like a deadly thing.

"Hello, Unc" was all she could get through her dry lips. Just respectful enough not to earn a slap, but not too flirty. She was working on a new method—short and respectful.

The last few methods hadn't worked. The most recent was guilt. She spent hours in the mirror practicing her most pitiful expression. She thought looking up at him like a very small child might make him want her less. But it was a stupid plan. It only made everything worse.

Short and respectful wasn't going to work either, she quickly realized.

He was already in her bedroom.

• • •

The following day, Papa finally made his way back from a long haul, rest weary and delirious. Papa swept through the door like crisp fall air, and Missippi leaped for him, but she could only make out his figure. It was dark outside, and the little light in the living room came from a small lamp on the side table. He hurried to the locked closet where he hid his small television.

"Papa!"

"Hey, Sippi! I can't hardly see you," he said before lifting her high in the air. "My back! You're getting heavy, girl."

Missippi huffed in response.

"*All in the Family* is about to come on," he said, hurrying to the plug. "I drove in clear from Charleston without stopping to not miss a minute. Come on, Sippi! Let's watch together."

She hurried to his side and sunk into the couch right next to him. He was such a good papa.

• • •

Missippi woke from a violent nightmare that she couldn't fully recall. All she ever remembered was a foul-smelling man, her tiny twin bed, and so much pain. She wanted to go back to sleep, but she was afraid the nightmare might pick up where it left off, so she sat up.

The sound of Papa's snoring in the next room made her smile. She loved the sound of someone else in the house—creaking floors in the night, sink water running, even urine streams and flushing toilets. All the things other girls her age took for granted about their families were the things she longed for. As he snored, she smiled, visualizing his chest rising and falling. Then she rose from her bed and began dancing to the sound of his slow, steady snores. Twirling figure eights in her flowing nightgown. She felt light and full of fresh, lovely summer air—young, innocent, untouched.

The sun peeked through the pines like a spy trying to catch a glimpse of something pure. Her bedroom warmed quickly, wrapping her in amber and shards of orange. She began to sing as she twirled.

"Wipe up, cook, dust, sweep, scrub, wipe up, cook, dust, sweep, scrub, wipe up, cook, sweep, dust, scrub," she sang. "Wipe up, cook, dust, sweep, scrub, wipe up, cook, dust, sweep, scrub, wipe up, cook, sweep, dust, scrub, milk for free . . ."

Milk for free, she thought. Her gaze fell on her belly, and she realized it had nearly doubled overnight. She hurried to the bathroom mirror and balanced on the lip of the tub to get a full view of her swollen tummy. A few short months ago, her frame was straight up and down like a cut tree trunk. Now she was lumpy like a badly stirred tapioca pudding. She huffed at her reflection. There was really nothing to be done. On the way back to her bedroom, she thought of Evangelist. Wipe up, cook, dust, sweep, scrub, wipe up, cook, dust, sweep, scrub, wipe up, cook, sweep, dust, scrub. She could do that.

"Wipe up," she said to herself.

Evangelist had left an extra-large bottle of Pine-Sol under the kitchen sink. Missippi poured small pools onto the countertops, floors, and stove just like she'd seen Evangelist do. Then she began edging away at them until they left the house gleaming.

"Cook."

When she opened the kitchen cabinet, she found vinegar, vanilla extract, cornmeal, maple syrup, flour, salt, baking soda, black pepper, seasoned salt, garlic powder, shortening, paprika, nutmeg, and a wooden rolling pin.

The smell of vanilla extract and paprika turned her stomach. She pushed them to the very back of the bunch and pretended they weren't there. Basil and garlic-powder shakers had never even been opened, so she pushed them to the back, too. The vinegar was long expired. She'd forgotten it was there, but when she caught a whiff, she craved the burn in the back of her throat. She shot back a capful and another and a third until she coughed. She really had no idea what to cook. Frustrated, Missippi put up everything except the flour, shortening, and maple syrup. She only knew how to make one thing.

"Two-step biscuits," she said. "One step flour, two step shortening."

She lit a torn-off edge of the Sunday newspaper to spark on the pilot light and turn on the gas oven. An invisible cloud of toxic stink whipped her square in the face and hissed like a bothered snake. Then she poured a mound of flour into the shape of an ant bed on the counter and spooned a dollop of shortening into the center like a volcano. With her spidery fingers, she kneaded the mixture until it felt like Play-Doh. Then she rolled the ingredients into a thin, flat sheet. The lid of an old mayonnaise jar cut out twelve perfect circles. She set the timer to twenty-five minutes.

"Dust."

She didn't own a duster. A too-small pair of stockings would have to work. Starting in the living room, she climbed on the tip-top of the couch and dusted the thick, wooly blanket from the top of the box fan in the window. Each blade held years of dead skin and hair and miscellaneous muck. Missippi had never noticed it before. She would've felt bad about it, but no other soul had ever told her to feel bad about that type of thing. Until Evangelist, that is. While dusting, she thought of Evangelist and Izella and Ola. Then: "Sweep."

The dust that had fallen on the floor was so thick that

it swept up easily. Sweeping was her favorite of the chores. Quick, easy, over.

"Scrub."

She dipped the steel wool from under the bathroom sink into the Pine-Sol and set to scrubbing the tub. Definitely her least favorite of the chores. The stubborn tub ring held on for dear life—deep dirt, dead skin, God only knows what. Whenever she broke the tub ring, instead of wiping away easily, it dispersed into gooey brown smears. And then when she went to wipe at the smear, it, too, dispersed. Smears caught like cooties.

As she finally got the tub gleaming, the ding of the timer sounded, and the smell of two-step biscuits filled her small house from crawl space to attic.

• • •

Missippi's papa woke up grinning at the smell.

"Hey, Sippi," he said in a slow drawl, wiping at his eyes. "Stayed gone too long this time, didn't I?"

"Yes, sir, you did."

He looked around. "You've got this place looking mighty nice."

"Yes, sir," Missippi said to him, bouncing on the back of her feet. "I made biscuits and syrup for you, and they ready."

"I'd love some," he replied, a new concern all over his face. "Bring it to my chair if you don't mind."

Missippi jumped to it, proud and happy for someone to feed. She stood in the middle of the clean kitchen and breathed deep to take it all in. She then stacked four of the biggest biscuits on a plain white plate and drizzled perfect rows of syrup overtop, then gathered ten ice cubes in both hands and dropped them into a tall glass of water one by one.

"One, two, three, four, five, six, seven, eight, nine, and ten," she chirped. "I hope you're hungry!"

Missippi's smile melted away when she saw her father sitting back in his chair with worry all over his face. "What's wrong, Papa?"

"Sit down here, Sippi." He patted the empty love seat to his left. She sat and he continued. "I stayed gone too long."

"Yes, sir."

"I'm not a good papa."

"You're the best papa in the world!" she told him, shocked at the sadness in his voice. He had a plate of fresh biscuits steaming in front of him. The floor was shining, and his glass of water was sweating cold. "What is it?"

Papa pointed at Missippi's big belly. "Who did this to you, Sippi? That boy across the way? Or Mr. Turner's child with the white lightning on his breath?" Her papa's head fell forward into his large hands. "Who would do this to a baby?"

"Can't say who, Papa," she said, concerned for her father. "He said I can't tell nobody. Not you most of all, Papa."

"Mississippi," he said in a shaky but stern voice. "You tell me right now who did this to you."

She shook her head until she gave herself a headache. The rules were clear. Don't. Tell. Your. Papa. He was a good papa—kind, calm, loving. She felt sorry for him. All alone on the road all the time with nobody to talk to. Her papa didn't deserve to die, and Unc said he'd kill him if he knew what was what. Papa could ask a million, gajillion times, but she wouldn't open her mouth.

"You haven't touched your two-steps, Papa."

"You ain't gone tell me, are you?" Papa asked. "I can see it all over you that you ain't gone tell me."

She shook her head and smiled wide. "No, sir."

"You can't tell who? I won't ask who. I'll ask other questions."

Missippi began to bounce in her seat. "Like a game?"

"That's it," he said, forcing a tight grin. "A game."

"Go!"

"Does he come here to this house sometimes?" he asked, clenching his fists into giant balls. "When I'm away?"

"Two questions, Papa!" she said in a high pitch. "You cheat."

"Does he come here when I'm away?" he snapped, and then softened. "See, I made it into one."

"Yes, sir," she said before stuffing one of his untouched biscuits into her mouth. "Only when your rig is gone."

"Do I know him?"

"You know everybody, Papa."

"How long has this been going on?"

"I don't know," she said before taking another big bite. "Few months. No! I know! First time was just after my thirteenth birthday down at the church, remember? You got Mrs. Minni to make me a cake, and you lit a candle on it."

"He go to church with us?" her papa asked with a tremor in his cheek.

"Yes, sir," she told him. "But sometimes he plays hooky from Sunday school."

"Is it Mr. Yancy's boy?"

"Yuck! No, sir!"

"Mrs. Oliver's son?"

"Papa!" she hollered. "His head is big as a melon!"

"Sippi," he said calmly. "Is this something you wanted to do? I mean, liked to do with a boyfriend?" He looked away so she couldn't see his eyes filling with large, involuntary tears.

"Ew, no." Missippi shuddered. "He old."

"Is he old as me?" he shouted, tears instantly dried.

Missippi chuckled. "How old you, Papa?"

"Mississippi!" He dropped his facade at the immediate realization that his daughter was not simply playing around with a boy her age. "Stop this game. Does this man look as old as me?"

"No, sir." Missippi squinted at her father's face. "Older."

"Older!"

Missippi was startled by her father's anger. She hadn't expected it. Unc told her what he was doing was all right. To her, it felt nasty, but he was older than her papa. And older folks supposed to know what's what in the world.

"Yes, sir."

"How much older is he than me?"

"I," she said, hesitant to speak or smile or move or breathe, "can't say, because I don't know how old you are, Papa."

"Forty-three!"

"I . . . Papa," she started. "You ain't gone gray. He's salt-and-pepper gray in the beard and chest."

Papa picked up the remaining plate of two-step biscuits and threw them at the newly scrubbed box fan, shattering all of it.

•••

"Bags packed?"

"Yes, sir," Missippi replied to her father. "Ready!"

He'd given her a week to pack up, but it only took a half day. She didn't have much—four outfits for in, and four outfits for out. A brush, a soap bar, two slices of green from the aloe plant, a picture of her mama, and the half-empty bottle of Pine-Sol, just in case she needed to clean up where she was going. Papa hadn't told her where he was taking her or for how long she'd be gone. He hadn't said much of nothing since he threw the biscuits. He just paced back and forth and back and forth again, mumbling the names of salt-and-pepper-gray men at church. Missippi hadn't realized how many there were.

Missippi had never seen her papa angry before. Usually, he was full of calm like a pigeon on a line. But no matter what Missippi cooked, Papa wouldn't sit or even sleep. He walked new holes in his socks, racking his brain. He kept asking Missippi who. She kept shaking her head. He never got angry at her, though. Kind, sweet, calm Papa. He was a good papa after all.

Missippi was excited to leave the tiny house behind. She longed for adventure and new faces, but she'd miss her little kitchen with the tricky gas stove, and the creaking spot in the hallway hardwoods, and even the pesky ring around the tub. She'd miss the mailman and the milkman and the iceman. But most of all, she'd miss watching Izella and Ola walking back and forth, skipping cracks, and twirling.

"Sippi," Papa said with pity in his sleepy eyes. "Time to go."

"Hold on, Papa," she told him before jogging to her room. "I have to say my good-byes! Bye, bed. Bye, side table. Bye, window. Bye, bathroom mirror. Bye, you ole nasty tub ring. Bye, stove. Bye, sink. Bye, icebox. Bye, couch. Bye, Pecola . . . No, Pecola, you're coming with me!"

She tucked the paperback novel into her skirt and leaped to her papa's side. "Now I'm ready."

• • •

Missippi had expected an adventure. She was excited to ride in the eighteen-wheeler with her papa, talking into the evening, sipping orange juice, and eating salt-and-vinegar potato chips. But the rig was just as lonely as the house. Papa had made her a sleeping slab in the back with the shelves and shifting boxes, and the only light was small enough to fit in her palm. His boss wouldn't allow another soul along on his long hauls, so Missippi couldn't even see him, let alone speak to him.

The trip took two full days, and the motion of the rig

left her belly spinning around and around. By the time they made it to where they were going, her whole body ached—swollen feet to swirling mind.

Papa lifted the rolling door, and the wind hit her like a slap.

"We here, Sippi," said Papa through a small grin. "Come on out."

Missippi rubbed at her eyes while they adjusted to the light. The wind was high and strange like in *The Wizard of Oz.*

A small-framed woman with hot-combed, shoulder-length hair covered in a silver scarf tied under her chin appeared next to Papa. Her expression was one of caution, almost fear, but not quite. She wore dark brown layers underneath a heavy wool coat. It was too hot for layers, Missippi thought. Such a strange and blanketed woman.

"This is Ms. Pearline," Papa told Missippi. "You'll be staying with her until what happens happens."

"How long, Papa?" Missippi pleaded. "I'll miss you."

"Soon, Sippi." Papa held out his hand and turned his face away to hide his eyes. "I'll come by when I have to drop a load off nearby."

Papa hugged his daughter tight and walked swiftly to the driver's side of the idling rig. He honked the giant horn twice before speeding out of the parking lot. When her papa disappeared around the corner, she caught a full view of her temporary home.

Missippi ducked when a train zipped high above a squatty, brown brick building. The train nearly ran smack into the tallest apartment she'd ever seen. Her eyes were saucers. Her mouth gaped.

She spun around like Izella on a hot, happy day. The world was a strange place, she thought. Her life last week was a living room, and now her world was a tall building, and an even taller building, and traffic lights, and so many cars everywhere, and oh, a playground full of kids. She'd never seen so many kids. Swinging high as the train. Licking frozen red Popsicles. Chasing each other around the sliding board.

Her first mind told her to run to them. Ask them to play with her and smile until they loved her as much as she already loved them. But then she remembered her aching feet and belly. And after that, she remembered the blanketed woman, Ms. Pearline.

Missippi looked around for her. The woman had gone as quickly as she'd appeared. She reached for her bags, but they were also gone; the woman had taken them away. Missippi began to panic. Strange place, strange woman. No bags, no Papa. Fear crept in.

Missippi heard the soft yell of her name bouncing

between buildings. She couldn't pin down the origin of the sound—it echoed from left to right and up to down and windowpane to windowpane.

"Missippi."

She heard her name a bit louder, and she spun around, desperate to find the source. "Again!" she yelled.

"Missippi," the voice said. "Look directly up."

Missippi lifted her chin a bit.

"Higher!"

She lifted a tiny bit more, because she couldn't imagine anyone living any higher than that.

"Higher!"

On a whim, she threw her head all the way back, and, on the top floor of the tallest building she'd ever seen in her life, she saw four female figures waving down at her. When Missippi waved back, acknowledging them, they cheered.

"Come on up," called one of the girls.

"Twentieth floor!"

"Seventh door on the right!"

"We'll be waiting for you at the elevator!"

• • •

The elevator doors opened to three giddy girls with their hair all over their heads. They eagerly pulled open the gate to grab Missippi through. An arm slid around her waist and another arm around her neck. The third girl walked backward in front of her, making her way down the long hallway.

"How long?" she asked. "Five, six months?"

"At least six," said the girl on Missippi's left as she cupped her palm under the belly button. "Her belly button's popped."

"Ouch!" said Missippi as the strange girl tugged at her out belly button.

"Oh," added the girl to the right. "At least six. That button's all the way out."

Their faces were round and only a few years older than hers, thought Missippi. No way they were sisters, though. They looked nothing alike—one stout and deep dark, another tall and light, and the last muscly and in-between. Their wild hair made them look like excited flames. Missippi chuckled at the thought: three walking, flame-headed girls. She liked them immediately.

When they reached the seventh door on the right side, the three girls went in one by one, and Missippi saw them. Full bodied and swollen, every single one of them.

"I'm Lillian," said the tall one. "Three months."

"Mary," said the stout one. "Two."

"And Ruby," said the last. "Just about any day now is what Ms. Pearline tells me."

Missippi didn't cross the threshold. She stood watching as they scurried through the apartment door to Ms. Pearline's side.

Not a single glimpse of Ms. Pearline's skin showed, aside from her twitchy face and hands. Her fingernails were bitten so low that the beds puffed up raw like stuffed chicken breast. She looked like she smelled awful, and Missippi wanted to sniff her, just to see if she was right. Covered in tiny wool balls, drab, and nervous, she was definitely the strangest woman Missippi had ever seen.

The small apartment was equally strange, especially compared to the sad gray hallway with slightly worn carpet. It was as if she'd stepped into a whole different world dipped in color. The walls were covered in ripped strips of painted canvas. Small, splashy drawings on tiny sheets of loose leaf and crayon-colored pictures of girls' smiling faces—some intricately sketched by true artists and others thrown together haphazardly. But all filling their own empty space on the wall, together, transforming the space into a wonderland.

One extra-large bed covered with a beautiful, hand-knitted quilt dominated the living area. The bed was made meticulously, fitted sheet tucked tightly and pillows fluffed. The open kitchen was also in order: five sets of dishes, grouped by color—blue, green, yellow, orange, and bright pink. The only area Missippi could see that was out of order was the large wooden easel in the corner littered with paint and supplies. The stand held a painting in progress—a swollen-bellied girl wearing grease-stained overalls, standing confidently in front of the open hood of a Chevy truck. In the background, empty country and lush green woods with milking cows underneath the setting sun. Only the girl's head was unfinished.

Missippi took small steps toward the headless girl on the pulled piece of canvas. "This me?" she asked.

Ms. Pearline nodded timidly, as if terrified Missippi would take offense or hate it. Missippi looked at the other three girls. And they looked back at her like her reaction to the painting was the most important thing in the world. It felt like a big moment to her. Did she or didn't she like the picture the blanketed woman had drawn of her before even laying eyes on her?

She thought of the wind hitting her face when Papa opened up his rig. That wind was the changing of the tides, from low south to high north. Lonely life to not being able to walk a step without bumping bellies with another girl. The winds of a city so windy Papa said they named it the Windy City. She took a peek out the high-rise's window. Kids running circles around the playground like ants marching and chasing each other through blades of grass.

Farther off in the distance, she saw blue water and even higher buildings. The sound of the rushing train taking the place of crickets in the background of life. She really was Dorothy. This really was Oz—Chicago.

She stared back at the painting of herself. Standing up straight, fixing cars, and waiting for a head. She then looked at her new friends, Lillian, Mary, Ruby, and Ms. Pearline.

"I love that picture more than any picture I've ever seen in my whole life, Ms. Pearline," said Missippi in a noticeable drawl. "But who's gonna draw me on a head?"

They all laughed, even Ms. Pearline, who, seconds earlier, looked like she wanted to pass out from anticipation.

Ruby, the muscly one, broke through the laughter. "Dang, girl! You are country!"

They all fell out laughing even louder. They were going to get along just fine for however long they had each other.

• • •

Missippi was exhausted. The bed was even more comfortable than her own back home, and the room had just enough light to sleep but not so little to be scared of the dark. The knitted cover smelled fresh, like it had been dried on a line, and all four girls slept head to foot underneath it.

Missippi, however, couldn't stay asleep, since Ruby's defined calf muscle kept banging her in the forehead. She smiled at the close company. This was what she'd always wanted, people surrounding her at all times. Snoring, kicking, smelly people doing all of the things people did. But this was so much better than anything she ever could have imagined. These girls were just like her—young and puffed up in the middle.

Missippi rolled onto her back to stare at the gray ceiling. It was the only thing left in the room still drab. Every other inch was filled with vibrant color and warmth. Missippi tried to imagine what the other apartments looked like, all plain Jane and bare. She thanked her stars she wasn't in one of those apartments.

Grinning, she listened to her new world. The dominant sound was Lillian's breathing in and out like a lion on a hill. But just underneath it was the city. Zooming cars, honking horns, and a million people walking on sidewalks, going on about the business of their night. She thought about how happy she'd been whenever she caught a glimpse of Izella and Ola back home. All of the stories she'd made up for where they were headed and coming from. That was small peanuts compared to Chicago.

Rubbing at her eyes, Missippi eased out of bed and tipped toward the cracked window to look out. Even in the pitch of night, a few boys sat around the swings talking and cracking jokes and laughing. Where on earth were their mamas? Maybe they didn't have mamas. Maybe they were just like her, mamaless with papas gone on long hauls. She wanted to go down and see why one, two, three, four, five boys around her age were on the playground so late. No way they had mamas.

"Can't sleep?" Ms. Pearline startled Missippi, who was lost in her watching. "Sorry."

"No, ma'am," said Missippi too loudly and with too much excitement. "No reason to be sorry. Ruby kicks in her sleep a little."

Ms. Pearline covered a laugh. "Yes, I know that. They know that, too, which is why they put you next to her."

"I don't mind one bit, Ms. Pearline." Missippi smiled as she watched Ms. Pearline curiously. She still wore layers upon layers of clothes—a sleep dress with long johns underneath, a robe over them, and her head wrapped tightly to top it off. "Why you wear so many clothes?" Missippi asked innocently and without judgment.

"You, child"—Ms. Pearline gave a respectful bow—"have just asked the question so many people have wanted to ask me but never had the courage to."

"I'm sorry." Missippi checked her manners. "Was that wrong to ask that?"

"No, no, no." Ms. Pearline took a seat at the easel. "Just brave of you to say what's on your mind, is all."

Still, she chose not to answer. They sat in silence for a few moments while Ms. Pearline squeezed and mixed paints onto an already stained palette. A dark brown mixed with stark white, creating a soft tan color in the middle surrounded by a dash of black and green and yellow and red. As she mixed, Ms. Pearline sucked on a long, wooden paintbrush like it was a cigarette. She looked like the type of woman who needed a cigarette, Missippi thought. Nervous and squirrelly and all.

"Don't you smoke?" Missippi asked with a sincere smile.

Ms. Pearline removed the paintbrush from her lips and laughed again. "I quit when I started with the girls. Bad for babies, you see? They come out smelling like smoke instead of babies. And babies smell better than smoke or anything else in the world."

There was another moment of quiet as Ms. Pearline chose which of her brushes she wanted to use. Missippi watched Ms. Pearline's fleshy fingertips hover above brush tips, twiddling and twirling and then changing her mind over and over. She finally chose the skinniest and most worn of the brushes. A small, black, slick slit of wood with a pinprick of hairs sticking out of it. Ms. Pearline smiled at it like she was smiling at her oldest friend, and then she placed it in her mouth like she would a cigarette.

Missippi chuckled. "So now you smoke paintbrushes."

"That I do."

As she painted, Missippi looked out the window at the boys. "Where are their mamas?"

Ms. Pearline put down her paintbrush and took a seat on the sill next to Missippi. "Every mother isn't a good mother, Missippi."

"Ain't that the truth!" Missippi said too loudly. "This Evangelist down the street from me is a mama, and she cut me down like a blade of grass one day. I sure hope all mamas aren't like that mama."

"My mother was wonderful," Ms. Pearline said, staring at the boys on the swings. "A librarian. Smarter than any man. Anybody else in the world, really."

"Where is she now?"

"My mother passed away right before I moved to Chicago." Ms. Pearline pulled in her robes as if there had been a breeze.

Instinct told Missippi to drop it. Ms. Pearline seemed fragile about that, and Missippi certainly didn't want to make her feel bad.

"So," she said, changing the subject. "When you start taking in girls? It's real nice what you're doing here. Papa never could've known half what you know about swollen girls."

"I started doing this when I found out what really happens to girls like you when no one helps."

Again, instinct told Missippi to drop it. Not because Ms. Pearline seemed fragile this time, but because Missippi herself did. "Girls like you" brought up anger that Missippi didn't know was there, and "what really happens" made her scared. What *did* happen to *girls like her* if there was no Ms. Pearline? Poor Papa was always gone, and Evangelist was mean, mean, mean as a pit viper. She didn't want to know, Missippi thought. Maybe later, but not tonight. She turned her attention back to the boys.

"Not having a mama in Chicago looks like fun," she said. "It's not fun in Georgia, not having a mama."

"Glitter and gold are not the same thing, Missippi," Ms. Pearline told her as she started back painting. "Not ever."

Sleep caught up with Missippi, and she eventually made her way to bed so exhausted that even Ruby's kicking didn't wake her. She dreamed of a baby boy tucked tightly in a blue blanket. His laugh like wind chimes on a porch in the spring. It was a good dream, until it turned bad. It was that same nightmare she couldn't quite remember. A foul-smelling man. Her tiny twin bed. And so much pain.

Then the dream changed again into screaming, wailing, yelling. Piercing hollers like nothing she'd ever heard in her fourteen years walking on earth. She felt wetness with her hands. Cold and callous wet. She pulled the knitted blanket for warmth, but it didn't help. Missippi's teeth chattered her awake. She shot from the dream, thankful that it was over. And then she found out that it wasn't a dream at all.

The screams she'd heard were real.

They were Ruby's screams. Her "any day now" had come.

• • •

Ms. Pearline crouched between Ruby's sweaty knees as Lillian and Mary held a thick stick in her teeth.

"Missippi," Ms. Pearline said in a gracefully calm voice. "On the counter, by the pepper grinder, you'll find a timer shaped like a chicken. Go get it and come back to Ruby's left side."

Missippi jumped up, nearly tripping on her way to the kitchen. Frantic, she kept overlooking the timer. The light brown pepper grinder, the handmade soap by the sink, the wildflowers stuck in an old tin can, stick-figure drawings and sketches. Everything in the world except the chicken timer.

"Missippi," Ms. Pearline said over Ruby's yelling. "Breathe."

As soon as Ms. Pearline spoke the words aloud, Missippi realized she hadn't taken a breath in some time. She'd nearly passed out from it, panting and coughing just like Ruby. Then she saw the timer. "Aha! I found it!"

She had no clue how she'd missed it. It sat right where Ms. Pearline had said it would be sitting—next to the pepper grinder on the counter. She grabbed it and hurried back to the living room.

"I want you to set that timer for ten minutes," Ms. Pearline said, staring into Ruby's crotch. "I'm speaking to you, Missippi."

"Oh! Me." Missippi went to twist the timer, but she was shaking so violently that it took more time than it should have. "Ten minutes, got it."

"Breathe," said Ms. Pearline. "Again, I'm speaking to you, Missippi—and pay attention to what's happening. This is where life begins. Painful. Beautiful life. Do not be afraid of it."

Missippi watched Ms. Pearline, crouched down, smeared with pee and bloody goo, but more calm than she'd ever seen her. All nervousness gone. She'd also shed her layers of clothing. Now that Ms. Pearline was without coats or robes or head wraps, Missippi could see the woman unblanketed. She wore only her white slip.

Ms. Pearline was the most stunning human being Missippi had ever seen up close. Arms so thin she could fit her fist around them, Missippi thought. Legs shapely and lean like a runner's. Hair the color of a brick, and wild like a flourishing fern. Even her toes were beautiful and long, like claws grabbing hold of a branch. The most amazing thing about Ms. Pearline, though, above all: her skin. It looked like she'd soaked in stars for years and years and come out glistening. Her skin picked up any light. Even in the near dark, a thin reflection of a streetlight found its way to the crease of her forearm, the half-full moon rested on her forehead, and the dim lamplight spotlighted only her, as if the rest of them weren't worthy of it.

Ms. Pearline reminded Missippi of an alien. Maybe she was one, sent to earth to take care of "girls like her" who would otherwise be lost to God knows where. Maybe, on her planet, "girls like her" didn't have to worry about Uncs and Evangelists and stubborn old rings around bathtubs. Missippi wanted to go back with her. She opened her mouth to ask Ms. Pearline if she could go, but caught herself. She was a crazy girl with crazy thoughts that didn't make any sense in the real world.

"Missippi," said Ms. Pearline. "How much time has passed?"

"Four minutes have passed." Missippi felt proud to answer the question correctly.

Ruby yelled out, and Lillian and Mary secured the thick stick between her teeth.

"Yell into this, Ruby," said Mary. "No yelling out."

"Thin walls," Lillian added. "Doing great there, gal."

Ruby nodded at Mary first, then Lillian, and then Missippi, which made her feel like a part of the circle. She loved that feeling.

"I'm about to examine you internally," Ms. Pearline told Ruby. "Ready?"

Lillian and Mary shut their eyes tight and held on to the stick.

"Ready," Ruby panted.

Missippi watched Ms. Pearline stuff what looked like her whole arm into Ruby's private place. Ruby cringed and wriggled like she desperately wanted to scream out.

"You haven't dilated at all, Ruby girl." Ms. Pearline slowly removed her hand. "But your cervix is fully thinned."

Lillian and Mary grinned and shook Ruby's arms encouragingly. They knew what thinned cervix and dilated meant, but all Missippi heard were words. It reminded her of the chunks of names in the Old Testament. They could go on and on for a whole chapter about whose son was whose daughter and whose brother was their son's son. Missippi never skipped over them, though. She sounded them out and said them aloud, because they were actually people who had lived and deserved to be called out. Cervix meant something important, Missippi thought, dilated, too.

Ms. Pearline must have read her mind. "Cervix is here." She placed her hand onto Ruby's low belly. "Any other day, it's about the size of a second finger, but today, for Ruby, it's wide, thin, and ready for baby."

Missippi smiled. "Baby rides it down like a sliding board?"

All four, including Ruby, chuckled at the question. "That's one way to put it, yes," Ms. Pearline replied.

"And dilate." Missippi was eager to soak up the moment. "What's that one mean?"

"Hold on a minute." Ms. Pearline focused all of her attention under Ruby's nightdress. "Breathe through this one, Ruby. One, two, three, breathe in deep. Okay, now out. Open your eyes; look at me. Breathe in with me. One, two, three, breathe in deep. Okay, out through your nose. You're ready for the tub. Lillian, go run the water.

Mary, stay there holding the stick tight. Get ready to set your timer, Missipi. In three, two, one, set it now."

Ms. Pearline wasn't nervous at all, Missipi noticed. Her hands weren't shaking, and her chest wasn't all jumpy. Actually, she seemed energized by the chaos.

"Good girl, Ruby. You can rest a few minutes," Ms. Pearline said as she rubbed lotion into Ruby's left foot and turned her attention to Missipi. "Dilated means the cervix has opened enough for baby to come through. Hold up your ten fingers."

Missipi gently placed the timer at her side and lifted all ten fingers into the air. Ms. Pearline began pulling her fingers down one at a time. "One centimeter dilated. Two centimeters dilated. Three centimeters dilated . . ."

She kept going all the way until she reached the last finger. Missipi loved being touched by female warmth and beauty. Every time Ms. Pearline touched a new finger, Missipi felt joy deep down in her guts. The pure bliss of a mamaless girl being told what was what by an earnest woman. She'd thought she wanted a mama like Evangelist, but she now realized she was wrong. She wanted a mama like Ms. Pearline. A smart mama who spoke well and didn't judge young girls with swollen bellies. An artist who knew about culture and pepper grinders and cervixes.

"Got it?" Ms. Pearline asked with a small, tepid grin.

"It's important that you know every bit of this." She glanced down at Missippi's stomach. "I think you might be having two."

• • •

As Ruby lifted her nightdress and squatted down in the tub filled with warm water, lavender, and clover, Missippi thought of two.

When Ms. Pearline smiled at her and said the word *two*, Missippi accepted, for the first time, that meant two babies. Two is usually a good thing. Two shoes, two hands, two-step biscuits. But two babies was a lot for anybody, especially a fourteen-year-old girl.

She thought about Mrs. Dixie at church, who was married to a deacon and carrying around a bonnet-headed monster of an arm-baby named Daisy. She was cuter than any baby in the wide world, Daisy was, but she was also meaner than a bed rail sticking out. Covered, tiny head to tiny foot, in pink lace and eyelet, that child would slap the daylights out of any man or girl that dare come near her. Missippi had once seen Daisy snatch a wig off the head of a church mother and hold it so tight God himself couldn't take it away. Poor Mrs. Dixie, one Daisy had given her a full head of gray and permanent lines between her eyes. Two Daisies would've killed her dead.

"This helps," Ruby said through clenched teeth. "Add in a little more hot."

Lillian turned the hot water lever to a trickle, and Ruby's eyes rolled back into her head. The heat must've given her a fair amount of relief.

"I need to check your dilation, Ruby." Without hesitation, Ms. Pearline lowered herself into Ruby's tub, and her hand disappeared into the water. "Four centimeters dilated. Good girl. Baby should be here by morning."

Ms. Pearline then stepped out of the tub, the bottom of her slip covered in pinkish slime, but she didn't even bother to wring it out. She knelt by Ruby's side, seemingly unbothered by it.

After that, the contractions came thick and fast. Ruby kept asking Lillian to warm her cooling water back up, and Mary took a wide-tooth comb and green grease to Ruby's scalp. All three speaking positivity and love over her.

"You're doing it, Ruby."

"Almost there."

"You look beautiful, girl."

Then came the neighbors. In succession, one after the other after the other, ladies from next door and down the hall and a few floors down to the left showed up with freshly knitted booties and bonnets. Others came with chicken and dressing, and cabbage filled with salt pork, and baskets of blueberries. But the main unit was the five of them—Ms. Pearline, Lillian, Mary, Ruby, and Missippi.

Missippi wanted to cry as she watched them. She had always loved watching people walk by her small house back in Valdosta. Making up stories about where people were coming from and going to. But she never could've imagined a love so pure as this. Love conquering pain and anguish. Love pushing out hate. Love banding together to splash color onto the gray and the drab.

Missippi wanted to cry so badly that she allowed herself to.

• • •

Ms. Pearline was right. By morning, a baby boy had come into the world, and just like Missippi's dream, he was wrapped up in a blue blanket. His voice, however, didn't sound at all like wind chimes in the spring. He was a screaming little something.

"He won't take it, Ms. Pearline." Ruby cried all morning like a sad camel. "He don't want my ninnies."

Ms. Pearline, still calm and completely collected, rubbed Ruby's feet and smiled. "He's an hour old. Give him time, my love."

"How long?" Ruby asked frantically. "He hates me."

Ms. Pearline gently placed Ruby's foot on top of a stack of pillows and went to her side. "Take your shirt off, and his, too."

Missippi wondered if she ought to look away. Naked breasts were not the norm where she was from, after all, but she stared as Ms. Pearline placed the tiny, yelling baby boy on Ruby's lower belly. "A few short minutes ago, this was his home." She placed Ruby's shivering hand under his naked behind and her other hand on her own breast. "Babies are born who they will become. This baby will grow up to be an independent man. Let him find his way to your breast himself."

Ms. Pearline stepped back and joined Lillian, Mary, and Missippi as they all watched the nameless little boy rooting around for his mother's nipple.

"It's called the breast crawl," Ms. Pearline whispered, as if not to disturb him on his search. "See? His face is going side to side and now up and up. It's a reflex in every baby. Some more than others, but they all have it. He wants to find his own way. Forge his own path."

Missippi could hardly believe her eyes as an hour-old baby slowly inched to Ruby's nipple and began to suck.

• • •

On his two-week birthday, baby boy still had no name. Lillian called him Red, since he was always hollering bloody murder, while Mary had given him the nickname of Scooter for no reason at all. Ms. Pearline and Missippi agreed to call him Baby Boy until Ruby herself came up with something. It was, after all, her baby to name.

"I can't think of nothing," Ruby kept saying.

She was the saddest girl Missippi had ever seen. It was so strange. Ruby was chipper and young before she'd had her baby boy, but after, she turned blue. Missippi tried asking what was what with her. She only shrugged in response. Ms. Pearline called it the baby blues. Mothers get that after they push out all the hormones, she said. It seemed that Ms. Pearline had a name for everything Ruby was going through. Even her hair coming out in the front had a name—alopecia, the quick loss of hair after giving birth.

Ms. Pearline made Missippi want to know more about everything. She was a woman who knew what she was talking about, and Missippi would love to be one of those kinds of women one day.

Missippi followed Ms. Pearline to the easel in the corner to watch her finish up a painting of Baby Boy wrapped in blue and surrounded by kites and sailboats. It was a painting that belonged in a little boy's room and then in his keepsake box, where it should never be lost or sold or given away to thrift. It was a masterpiece, just like he was.

A single knock at the door shocked everyone to attention. Lillian and Mary stood, flanked at Ruby's and Baby Boy's sides like guardian statues. Ms. Pearline closed her coat tight around her and began to shake. She was nervous again, Missippi thought. Her calm was replaced by the opposite of calm. And then the baby began wailing.

Ms. Pearline walked cautiously to the door. "Who's there?"

"Ruby's granny!" a woman yelled from the other side of the closed door. "Come to see my grandbaby."

Ms. Pearline turned to Ruby with such sadness in her eyes. Missippi wanted to tell her not to open the door. Let the woman stand outside where she belonged. This was Ruby's family now. She didn't even know if Ruby's granny was good or bad or mean or sweet, she just knew that she didn't want any outsiders inside. Their union was forged and earned. No one else had any right to sit at the foot of their bed. No right to lay their foreign eyes on their Baby Boy. Blood was thinner than water in that place.

Ms. Pearline opened the door to reveal a stout woman in a flowery dress and hat. She looked like she could bake delicious cookies. Like a granny from a storybook or a fairy tale, a good one at that.

"Where's my great-grandbaby?" She spoke in an upbeat peep that matched her appearance. "Where is my little man?"

She made a slow beeline to Baby Boy, and Missippi's instinct was to pounce on her flowery throat. When the woman lifted Baby Boy from Ruby's arms, Missippi felt her nostrils flare and mouth clench up. She loathed this kind-looking woman with an unexplainable passion.

"Get your things, Ruby," the woman said, staring at Baby Boy with so much love in her eyes that she looked like she might burst. "Let's take this sweet baby home."

Missippi jumped up, unable to control her anger. "No!" she yelled. "You can't just waltz up in here and take our Baby Boy off somewhere. This is his home, lady!"

"Missippi." Ms. Pearline went for her arm.

"No!" She wouldn't allow Ms. Pearline to finish. "We can't let this happen."

Lillian and Mary tried to stop hysterical Missippi, but there was no calming her. She was a wild bull let loose. "It's not right, y'all! Why are you just standing there and letting this happen?" Missippi began to cry inconsolably. "You can't take them away. You can't."

"Come here, you," Ruby said to Missippi with a sad smile. She held her hands open as Missippi fell into her. "I'll miss you more than you know. I'll miss all of you."

Lillian and Mary joined the hug clump and also began to cry.

"This part doesn't get easier, does it?" Lillian asked Ms. Pearline, who was shaking and frazzled in the corner.

"Never," she replied before joining the hug. "If anything, girls, it only gets harder."

• • •

Ruby and Baby Boy left Ms. Pearline's apartment on a clear blue Sunday afternoon. Missippi cried a flash flood until the sun rose on Tuesday.

"Where'd Ms. Pearline go off to?" Mary asked, still mourning. "She's been gone since last night."

When the streetlights blinked off, Missippi began to worry. "Should we go out looking, y'all?"

"Yes," Lillian replied sarcastically. "Three big-bellied detectives searching Chicago for a woman covered in coats in the dead of summer. They'll lock us all up in the crazy house."

Missippi knew she was right. They were all showing now. No way they could go out without everyone asking questions.

Then the key turned in the lock, and two figures appeared in the doorway. One, blanketed Ms. Pearline, and the other was even more covered up. A quilt covered the second girl's head, and opaque stockings blocked legs. Missippi couldn't make heads or tails of it. She searched the second figure for clues, and she saw the bottom tip of an acoustic guitar covered in flower stickers and branded peace signs.

"Uh," Missippi said. "Ms. Pearline, who is this?"

"This," she replied, "is Susan. It's okay now; you can take the blanket off. It's safe."

Missippi, Lillian, and Mary gasped when they saw her.

Dirty-blond pixie cut, pink cheeks, and holding two fingers in a peace sign.

"Hi," she said to them. "They call me Sue for short. A girl named Sue." She laughed a little and then stopped.

They all stood silent, mouths gaping.

In the highest peak of the tallest tower, in the middle of Chicago, stood seventeen-year-old Susan. Ms. Pearline's very first white girl to come to the apartment.

"Come on in, Sue," said Ms. Pearline before wrapping her arm around her. "Let's get you something to eat."

SUE

11 Weeks—A Few Days Prior

The streets of Washington, DC, filled with all kinds of people holding on to pictures of blown-up little kids.

Sue didn't understand how anyone could support such a war. Kids were kids, whether from San Francisco or North Vietnam. Kids were clueless about life and war and death. Or they should be, anyway. They should be whole and innocent and free of worry.

It was an emergency protest, organized by the National Peace Action Coalition, Sue's favorite group of people in the whole world. Her high school's chapter, back in Kenilworth, Illinois, was led by the most passionate boy on earth, Michael Matthews. His longish hair and skinny waist made Sue swoon, but it was his zeal for justice that made her love him. If he had said it needed to be done, she would've done it. Absolutely anything for Michael Matthews. So when he told her to get on a bus to DC with him, she packed up her guitar and got on a bus to DC.

The week before, they'd been writing letters to senators, including her baby-killing father, Senator Day from the great state of Illinois. Then, after a lengthy bus ride, they stood in the midst of history in Washington, DC. A coming together of souls in support of the human race. Sue couldn't stop smiling.

In the crowd, she spotted a yellow flower about to get stomped by an angry protester. "Hold up, Mikey!"

She kissed him, put down her guitar, and ran to the flower, elbowing and excusing herself to reach it. She covered the tiny burst just before it was about to be crushed, picked it up, and placed it on the helmet of an armed officer.

"Peace to you," she told him with a smile.

"Fucking hippie," he spat in response.

She pranced back to Michael's side and tuned her guitar. "What should I play?" she asked him. "They're getting angrier. Maybe something mellow."

"Anger is necessary, Sue," Michael sputtered. "Don't be naive. Look at those pictures over there. If you're not angry, you're not paying attention."

Sue shook her head. "I can't see any more pictures of kids like that. It turns my stomach."

"It fucking should."

Sue ran through her mind, searching for the perfect song to sing. Joan Baez was her hero. Sue cut her hair the same week Joan did. Taught herself guitar when she first heard "I Live One Day at a Time" and "Joe Hill." She didn't have Joan's vibrato or her lower register, but she'd do her best.

"I dreamed I saw Joe Hill last night, alive as you and me. Says I, 'But Joe, you're ten years dead . . .'"

A small crowd formed around her. A few left crowns of flowers, and some even flicked coins her way. She sang from her low belly. The song wasn't right unless she felt it rising up from inside. When she reached the end of the short song, she was out of breath. Singing from her heart exhausted her thin body.

"Can we hear another?" encouraged a sweet-faced, older woman wearing tie-dye.

"How about 'Chelsea Morning' by Joni Mitchell?" asked a middle-aged man in bell-bottom jeans.

Sue was afraid of "Chelsea Morning." It was too high for her, and she never sang a song she couldn't do justice. Music was life, and as a musician, Sue knew when someone believed what they sang. Both Joans believed it—Joan and Joni—and so did she. A song as beautiful as "Chelsea Morning" deserved to be believed in by its singer.

A nervous rumble came up from her stomach, and Sue was shocked by its power. Reverberating through her body were tremors of anxiety. She rarely felt this way. After what seemed like thousands of talent shows and impromptu sidewalk performances, Sue was a professional at this. She'd worked out all of her fear over time and never got nervous anymore. Was she coming down with something? she wondered. She froze with fear as the small crowd began to chant.

"'Chelsea Morning,' 'Chelsea Morning,' 'Chelsea Morning . . .'"

She looked over to Michael for help, but he, too, was chanting along with the crowd. Dizzying, mind-numbing confusion tilted her understanding of the world, and she thought she might faint. Her dry mouth began craving wetness. Water, she thought. Someone please get her water now.

The sidewalk lifted, and the large crowd blurred into bouquets of color—red, white, green, blue, yellow. She swallowed a giant lump of air in a gulp and felt it coming back up. A rising and rising from the low place she sang from. She hadn't eaten at all. There was nothing to come up. Nothing but swallowed air and music.

"'Chelsea Morning,' 'Chelsea Morning,' 'Chelsea Morning . . .'"

In that moment, Michael caught the plea in her eyes and tilted his head. *What's wrong?* he mouthed.

But it was too late. She threw up on the tie-dye lady's open sandal.

The world settled after that. The bouquet of colors turned back into a sea of people, the sidewalk lay back down, and the wetness coated her mouth again. She squeezed her eyes shut once and then opened them wide to get her bearings. The disgusted woman stood in front of her, shell-shocked by the vomit on her bare toes. The rest of the small crowd had dodged it and scattered.

Sue looked from the woman's outraged face to the vomit on her foot. It was bright yellow, like Joni's "Big Yellow Taxi."

"You okay, Sue?" asked Michael, who was also keeping a safe distance from her.

"What's today?" she asked him.

"Saturday."

"No," Sue snapped. "I mean the date."

The frozen woman with the newly yellow toe said, "May twenty-seventh, 1972."

Sue simply replied, "Shit."

• • •

The next day, Sue and Michael rode the bus back to Kenilworth in silence. Well, mostly silence, except for the gagging coming from Sue. Her world revolved around sound, and on that bus, she heard herself as a chorus of an angry body, deciding, once and for all, to either accept the thing or push out the thing. It sounded like she herself was at war on the inside.

The bus didn't help. The driver seemed to aim for every uneven crack in the freeway and dodge everything smooth. Sleep evaded her completely. All she had was a miserable, bumpy, vomit-filled ride from hell.

Her mother would be furious. That much she knew. And her father, too, if he was even in Kenilworth. The protests kept him at the capital most days. Even during Senate recesses, he stayed in his Washington apartment. *For the sake of the country*, he'd tell her before kissing her on the cheek. She'd always wait until he was gone to wipe his spit off her face. Yeah, right, for the sake of the country. For the sake of war was more like it. She hoped he was still in Washington. He was the last person she wanted to see. Seeing her mother, though, worried her.

Sue's mother was a quiet woman named Margaret. Tall, slender, demure, she was raised in New England, right alongside the Kennedys. She'd been on the Vineyard when the Chappaquiddick episode happened. She'd told Sue about the late-night sounds of zooming police cars and so many blue and red lights that it looked like the Fourth of July had come around again. When her mother described "the incident," as she called it, she never allowed her voice to rise above a womanly whisper.

And as a rule, Margaret never let her hair or fingernails grow too much without being tended to, and she rarely kept a pair of shoes long enough to get scuffed on the bottom. To the world, she was a superior snob, and she never parted her lips to disagree. If her mother were an instrument, she'd be a flute of a woman. Tinkering and adding airy, breezy flavor to the symphony. Sue, herself, was a proud acoustic guitar. Even Sue's father treated his wife like a fancy pocket square to give a pop of expensive color to his suit. Sue, however, knew who she really was.

Sue's mother was the queen of thought commentary. She

whispered her anger into her tea and secretly donated money to the brand-new National Public Radio station called WBEZ. She was the fiercest of women, quietly making differences no one would ever know about. Polar opposite of her father, Sue thought. He was a show pony, prancing around to white-tie dinners with crooked Richard Nixon. Holding the president's umbrella in perfect weather for a chance to be photographed alongside.

Her mother, though, was the one who'd lit Sue's fire of activism. In 1968, she brought Sue to Chicago to witness the Democratic National Convention. When mayhem broke out, Sue expected her mother to retreat like everyone else. She didn't.

Dressed in low heels and a pink peplum dress, her mother, with perfect posture, stood her ground in the chaos. Sue was just thirteen years old, tugging at her mother's ruffles, but she wouldn't budge. That's when Sue realized how much her mother despised the war, and maybe even her own husband. Even still, everything Sue had learned about her mother, she'd done through observation. The woman rarely spoke outside of rehearsed niceties. Her mother was a bag of pieces of a whole that she had to pour out and put together over the span of her life. Those big pieces, like the protest, were rare and welcomed, but usually, Sue made do with the tiny shards between manicures.

"You sleeping?" Michael's wiry voice broke through the bus's background noises.

"No," she replied. "I can't sleep."

"What are we supposed to do about this?" Michael said, all of his attractive confidence replaced by ugly apprehension. "I'm not ready for . . ." He looked around before continuing. "A child."

"Nobody's ready for a child," Sue replied, upset at the sound of him—boyish, squirrelly, scared. "Where did you put my guitar?"

"Who the hell cares where your stupid guitar is, Susan!" he said in a loud whisper before cowering under the gaze of the man one seat over. "My dad is going to kill me. And my grandmama." He placed the back of his hand on his forehead like a woman about to faint on a soap opera.

Just then, Sue felt the magnitude of her mistake. He was a pussy. A paper tiger. A kid in a candy suit pretending to politic. She wanted to vomit again, but on him this time. Sue wasn't afraid of pregnancy or her father or mother or anything else for that matter. The only thing that scared her, in that moment, was being attached to a snobby rich kid who'd been pretending this whole time.

To, God forbid, share a child and a home and a life with a boy like this. Her instinct was to dismiss him from her presence and never speak to him again. She'd done faker boys like that tens of times. But she was stuck. And that was the mistake.

She looked him over and felt a rumble in her stomach before saying, "Shit."

• • •

Guitar in hand, Sue walked through the front door to find her mother sipping tea in the front room. With pursed lips and a furrow between her eyes, she said, "Susan, sit."

Two words strung together from her mother's lips were a lot. She dutifully sat.

"Would you like a cup of tea?" she asked her daughter before lifting an empty cup from the side table and pouring. "Mint."

Sue took the tea in one hand, never fully releasing the neck of her guitar as a comfort. Thankful to be off the loud bus, Sue acclimated to the quiet. This was the life she grew up living. A soundless, expensive sipping of tea.

"Where did you go, Susan?" her mother's tea-burned

voice asked. "You were away for a day and a night. I worried."

Sue thought of telling her mother right there. Then she changed her mind about that, because she wasn't sure what would happen. The quiet ones were the scary ones, Sue thought. Those who sit and brood without blabbering on and on about everything could do the most damage with their words. People assumed they were blank and without opinion. No, they were the most thoughtful. Taking in every single detail of the world. Soaking it up. Devising plans and donating secretly to causes they cared about. To Sue, quiet meant strength of will. Control over one's self. When she really thought of it, the act of reacting was the weak act. Resistance of emotion was the real strength. And in that way, her mother was more powerful than God.

But then again, she'd seen the activist within her mother, hiding, but there.

"I missed a cycle last month," she decided to say to her with a phony confidence that made her think of Michael. "Pretty sure I'm pr-preg—" Sue stopped there, unable to say the word.

When her mother said nothing and showed no emotion whatsoever, Sue was uneasy. So she did what she always did when she felt out of sorts. Searched for sound. Honing in on the patter of her own heartbeat and the whistle of her breathing. Then searching for her mother's heartbeat and breathing. They were small sounds. Nearly unable to be heard at all. They needed a cat, she thought. Or a very small dog.

Her mother took another sip of tea.

"I'm sorry . . ." Sue began, but her mother held a manicured finger in the air.

"Let's not," she said simply. "I need time to think. You are excused."

• • •

Time to think is a tricky monster of a thing. It could mean anything, really. Time to devise a plan for how to get your daughter out of her predicament. Time to figure out how to kill your daughter without getting caught. Time to sip tea and eat an extra bite of shortbread cookie. It could mean anything in the world.

Sue squeezed the skinny neck of her guitar until her fist ached. She needed to play. As soon as her rear end hit the carpet of her bedroom floor, she began playing "Chelsea Morning." Too high and pitchy for public, but perfect for herself. Hearing herself squeal like a stuck pig, she truly didn't do Joni justice at all.

• • •

Sue woke to the sun shining in her eyes and attempted to flick the crook from her neck, since she'd foolishly used her guitar as a pillow. Her stomach rolled louder than a thunderstorm, and she wanted to cry. She began to play instead.

"How many roads must a man walk down, before you call him a man?"

Bob Dylan was a poet more than he was a singer. She'd never loved his voice that much. His lyrics, though, were utter magic. The strings of her guitar dripped tears by the time she reached the last line of the song.

"The answer, my friend, is blowin' in the wind. The answer is blowin' in the wind."

That song always teased out Sue's trapped emotions. Along with the tears, it drew out anger. Michael Matthews, passionate protestor, was actually a coward, worried sick about his grandmama. And the thing inside her was half his.

Sue had slept with six guys in her life. The first two were duds. The third, nice enough. And the fourth was a total loser. But the fifth, Malcolm Engel, should've been the father of this baby.

There was a small knock on Sue's cracked bedroom door, her mother's knock.

"You sang beautifully," said her mother, standing at the edge of the threshold, waiting to be invited in.

"Come in, Mother."

Her mother held her hands as she entered, one over the other, as if she'd practiced how to walk in the mirror. She took a seat on the chaise at the foot of Sue's bed and crossed her ankles. And then, quiet. Comfortable quiet, but quiet nonetheless.

This was why Sue had taken up the guitar. Raised in a large, hushed home, Sue had wanted to fill it with something else. Something interesting. Waves of sounds from pitchy Joni to slow, deep Johnny Cash. Her mother, in her way, encouraged it. A smile here and there—Sue thought her mother liked it. Besides, there was no pressure on her mother to speak or converse or add to dialogue. All she had to do was listen and nod as Sue played.

"You've missed how many cycles?" she asked after a while, forcing her lips apart like jackhammers.

"Two." Sue shook her head. "Maybe three?"

"Ahh," her mother replied, like she'd just heard that a squirrel had gotten into the attic.

"I'm sorry, Mother."

"I know."

A fly on the wall would've thought it strange—a

daughter telling her mother she's pregnant and the mother quietly taking it in. But this was how they were. It had always been the two of them quietly against the whole world. While her horrible father fought for his own political photo ops, they were there like this together. Always.

"I've thought of a solution," her mother said slowly, and then paused. Anyone else would've seen her as heartless, but Sue saw anxiety all over her. Sue knew she was about to say more than she wanted to, so Sue smiled and nodded, encouraging her mother to find her words.

"I . . ." her mother began, and then lost her words. "I . . ." she began again, and lost them again. "You . . ." She closed her lips into a tight line, and Sue knew her mother wouldn't open them again for some time. She needed to think.

"Want me to play while you think?" Sue asked, lifting her guitar to release some of the pressure from her mother.

Her mother nodded, seemingly grateful.

"I'll play your favorite.

"When you're weary, feeling small. When tears are in your eyes, I'll dry them all . . ."

"Stop," whispered her mother. The tears ran quickly

down her face like they would on a marble surface. She was crying. Sue had never seen her mother cry before.

"Mom," Sue started, but now she was at a loss for words.

Her mother scrubbed the tears from her cheeks and forced the words through her body. "You have to go away. Your father must not know. No one can know. Do you understand?"

Sue nodded in terror. Go where? How would this ever work?

"I help a woman," her mother continued. "A wonderful woman who takes in girls like you."

"Girls like me?"

Her mother shook her head, frustrated at her own phrasing. "This is why I don't speak. All things come out differently than I intend them to."

"It's okay," Sue replied, still stinging from the phrase "girls like you." "Please go on. You're doing well."

"She's on her way to retrieve you now." Her mother spoke through gritted teeth. "Your father will think you're at camp. He's preoccupied with the president, anyway." She spoke about him like she would a person she'd rather not exist. "Who is the father of this child?"

"Michael Matthews."

"Ahh," her mother said with a pinch of disgust. She

was no fan of the Matthewses. They were the type of rich people with golden faucets. Tacky rich. "Does he know?"

Sue nodded.

"Ahh," her mother replied again. "I'll have to handle them."

"Mom? Who is on their way to retrieve me?"

"Her name is Pearline. The place is small. Please pack only necessities. And there will be no phone where you're going, my darling," she said, blinking away emotion. "I will write."

• • •

The moment Sue had seen three other pregnant girls in the small, colorful apartment, she knew it was the right thing. No one slept that night. Not Lillian or Mary or Missippi or Ms. Pearline. The girls sat cross-legged on the bed and talked all night while Ms. Pearline frantically painted her pictures.

Missippi was immediately Sue's favorite. She loved her drawl and her innocence and her love of books. If Sue had a little sister, she'd want her to be Missippi—sugary sweet and curious about everything.

"Who's Johnny Cash?" Missippi had asked Sue in her unhurried twang.

"Who's Johnny Cash?!" Sue said, intentionally melodramatic. "Holy cow, let me show you."

She took out her guitar and began the song she knew they'd like. Everyone liked it. It was the most fun song to sing and play and listen to in the world. The song no one could hear without leaping to their feet and dancing: "I've Been Everywhere."

And Sue was right. All three girls got up and started twisting and laughing around the living room and kitchen as she sang. When she reached the first chorus of places, the girls threw their hands up and hollered.

"I've been to Reno, Chicago, Fargo, Minnesota, Buffalo, Toronto, Winslow, Sarasota, Wichita, Tulsa, Ottawa, Oklahoma, Tampa, Panama, Mattawa, La Paloma, Bangor, Baltimore . . ."

As the towns and cities rolled off her tongue, the girls shouted.

"She said Chicago! That's my city."

"Oh! I been to Tulsa! And drove through Tampa once."

"I'm from Baltimore! My hometown is in a Johnny Cash song!"

Sue smiled. No matter who she played the song for, she got the same reaction. People were simply excited that a song had their hometown's name in it. When she reached the end, they all clapped, and she bowed into her guitar.

“I like that Johnny Cash.” Missippi gave her the widest, sweetest smile Sue had ever seen. Sue wanted to grab her into her chest. She herself wasn’t much older than Missippi, three years and change, but Missippi’s pregnancy seemed wrong. Who would do this to such an innocent soul?

“Do you know old Chubby Checker?” Lillian seized Mary’s hand, and they began twisting together in the kitchen. “My mama loves him.”

“Mine, too! Ooo,” Mary added. “Play ‘The Twist’!”

“I’ve heard it, but I don’t know how to play that one.”

“Girl,” Lillian told her. “Do you know how to do the twist?”

Sue shook her head. Anxiety came back into her. She hated dancing. Actually, she never did it. Not even in private. She was a musician only; she created the music for other people to dance to. No, no, no. She would not dare dance in front of another soul. Not ever.

Lillian held her hand out for Sue. “Come on. It’s just us!”

“I can’t dance.”

“You may not be able to dance,” Lillian replied. “But you can twist them skinny hips. Get up!”

Mary began singing the chorus of “The Twist.” Sue had definitely heard that song before. It was an oldie, but a classic. She watched Missippi grinning and twisting with her way-out and out-of-place stomach.

Missippi was enormous. Bigger than all of them. Round and sticking out like two basketballs stuffed under her nightshirt. Younger, sweeter, and so much bigger. Sue felt the look of pity creep in between her eyes, and she quickly shook it off. Sue never wanted anyone to think she felt sorry for them. It was a complex she'd developed long ago as a rich girl.

A few years back, when Sue was barely a teenager, she'd wandered off on one of her downtown adventures. She was approached by an elderly homeless woman pushing a filled shopping cart. The woman had asked her for a dollar, but instead, Sue gave her a crisp twenty-dollar bill. "I'm sorry you don't have any place to live," she told the woman.

In response, the woman held the twenty high in the air and said, "If you're giving me this because you feel sorry for me, I'll give it right back to you. You reek of richness and pity." And then the woman hooked her neck back and spat to her left as Sue hurried off.

Sue had no idea what to say or how to handle that moment. As she'd passed her money along to the woman in need, she'd felt a surge of warmth and self-sacrifice shoot through her body. She was a do-gooder. Planting a seed within the community. She was surely someone who gave a damn about her fellow man. That was her last twenty—her bus or cab fare. Without it, she didn't know how she would get back to Kenilworth. Yet still, with the best of intentions, she'd offended.

From that moment, she decided that looking down her nose at anyone was a privilege not afforded to the well-off. People automatically assumed she would do it, so Sue went out of her way not to. Sue tried extra hard not to show those things on her face. Sometimes too hard probably.

Mary sang the chorus over and over like she didn't know the full lyrics. Sue almost picked up her guitar to strum along, but she decided what the hell. Go ahead. Throw caution into the wind. She got up and joined the circle of twisting girls.

"You weren't lying!" Missippi hollered. "Your knees are knocking!"

Lillian grabbed her hip bones and started manually moving them to the music, but it was no use. Sue's body couldn't be controlled. She was chronically offbeat. The girls fell into hysterics. Even Ms. Pearline stopped painting to chuckle from behind her easel.

Sue's mother was so right. This was the best place for her to have this child. Surrounded by laughter, love, and other young girls in her same predicament. How could her mother have known? A place of paint and music and self-sacrifice. Sue wanted to call her mother and thank her. She also wanted to walk right up to Michael Matthews and rip the peace patches from his jacket. He didn't deserve them. Sex with him wasn't even that good. He panted like an overheated dog.

Then she thought of her father. He would be furious if he saw. Not just the pregnancy part. That was bad enough, but the company surrounding her. Sue, herself, tried desperately to see people as auras of human energy, either positive or negative, never by the amount of pigment in their skin. To Sue, stereotypes of any kind were unfair. But her father, her horrible, horrible father, saw color first. If he saw where she was now, he'd shower the group with slurs, remove her, and forbid her ever to return. He'd judge them immediately as less-thans. Not worthy of his company or his daughter's.

The more she knew about the real world, the more she loathed her father's haughty guts.

• • •

They were supposed to sleep together in the large bed, head to foot, but that didn't happen. They fell out after the Johnny Cash twist party and talked all night long about life, love, and, most of all, the road that had led each of them to Ms. Pearline's twentieth-floor apartment.

"I thought I was in love," Lillian said before letting out a huff of air like an annoyed mare. "He was a fine one. Shiny shoes and a head full of grease." She laughed. "He never did let me touch his hair. Not once. Even while we were . . . you know. If this child looks like him, he'll be a fox, though."

"He was your boyfriend?" Missippi's voice was colored with wonder. When Lillian nodded in response, she continued. "How long y'all go steady?"

"Few months," Lillian replied, attempting to look unaffected. "I made him wait weeks, but he wouldn't leave me alone about it. Pesky bastard. It's all he ever talked about. He was a dog in after a bone, come to think of it. He was . . ."

Lillian trailed off without finishing her thought. It was as if she'd been swept into a memory she couldn't vocalize.

"What did your mother say?" Sue inquired. "When she found out."

Lillian laughed. "You just read my mind, gal. That didn't go well. My mother's a Seventh-day Adventist, you see? Didn't go well at all."

"Me, neither," Mary injected. "My mama broke every plate in the kitchen when I told her."

Missippi's head lowered when they talked about their mothers. Sue saw it, but she was the only one who had. Her instinct told her to change the topic.

"What about your boy, Mary?" Sue asked, turning her full attention toward her. "Boyfriend or playmate?"

"Where I come from there's no such thing as a playmate," Mary replied with a wink. "Doesn't go over in a town as small as mine. Everybody knows everybody's business. Boyfriend or nothing."

"How long?" Sue was still watching Missippi in her peripheral vision to make sure she was okay.

"Dennis has been my guy since fourth grade." Mary's voice perked up when she said his name. "Never missed a day without talking to him until I got here. I miss him more than a little bit."

Missippi sighed longingly. She was a girl who had never been loved by a boy, Sue thought. She wanted to ask her what her story was. It was her turn to speak, after all. The other two girls got caught up just like Sue had. From their stories, she surmised they'd had sex at the right moment of the month for egg to meet sperm, and there they were, cross-legged in Ms. Pearline's living room. But Missippi was an innocent. A baby giraffe wandering around clueless, malleable, vulnerable. She wouldn't dare ask her story. Not here, and likely, not ever. She had more respect for her than that. And if she wanted to tell it, she would.

"So, Missippi," Lillian jumped in. "Who knocked you up?"

Sue's quiet years at home with her mother had taught her to read body movements. Since her mother was stellar at hiding her outward emotions, Sue had become expert at it. A twitch of the nose here and a shrug of the shoulder there. Involuntary knuckle pops, ankles crossed against the right leg of the chair, and, above all, the unmistakable purse of the lips. Sue wanted to give Lillian a pass, because she surely didn't know what Missippi's body language meant. Sue could tell that Lillian was just teasing. She meant zero harm, but still, Sue wanted to punch her square in the nose for asking such an inappropriate question.

"I don't have a boyfriend to speak of," Missippi said in a low voice covered in glum.

Sue placed her hand on Missippi's thin knee. "You don't have to say if you don't want to."

Missippi looked grateful and shook her head. Just as Sue thought, she hadn't wanted to share. Lillian and Mary caught the drift and also dropped it.

They went on talking for hours about hometowns

and family and friends. Things they missed about home and things they'd hate to go back to. In the end, they even talked about the war. Uncles, fathers, brothers, cousins, and friends who'd come back different. Sue had to temper herself. She didn't want to express the depths of her hatred of Vietnam to them on the first night. Might scare them off like it had plenty of other potential friends.

Then came the question everyone wanted to know. Always.

"What's your daddy do, Sue?"

"Banker," Sue lied. "He's a banker at a bank."

He was anything but a banker. She always felt those questions—*who's your father, and what does he do?*—invasive. It loomed over her large house and her mom's fancy car and her sleepaway camp. Everyone wanted to know, no matter where she went, who her father was and what he did for a living. She stunk of being a girl with an important father. She'd always told the truth until that moment. Maybe it was because she really cared what these girls thought of her. Really, truly, wholeheartedly cared. For that reason, she lied through her teeth. What her father did was a complete, utter embarrassment to Sue. And she thought too highly of her new friends to let them know.

• • •

When Sue woke up, they were flailed on top of one another. Arms draped over, legs intertwined, heads on laps and shoulders. Somewhere in the night, Sue had sunk to the bottom of the pile. Trapped underneath girls she'd only met the day before. Sue caught a whiff of rotten eggs. One of the three girls had farted in her face, and she tried to hold her breath until it passed. It didn't pass. It was thick like a wool blanket, and lasting.

She tried to focus on something else. Then a memory flooded Sue's mind. Summer camp in Cambridge last year. The girls bunked four to a room, each in their own twin bed. Roommates were supposedly randomly assigned, but she was put with three other senators' daughters, which only amplified her father's influence. He'd wanted her to run with her own kind. To form a flock of politicians' kids like graceful geese in pearls. He was already pleased by the possibility of Sue marrying one of their brothers.

From day one in Cambridge, Sue knew she'd be an immediate outcast with her roommates. She skipped into the room, expecting three free-minded girls from other parts of the country. She'd expected some culture, art, music. But when she saw them, she saw only hair. Big, beautiful, well-cared-for hair. She smelled the burning of hair. Hair made its way into her potato chips. She fished it from the bathroom sink and tripped on curlers with hair left behind in them. It was a nightmare of a horrible summer of hair. The best she could do to pass the time was read and count days.

Ms. Pearline's apartment was what camp should've been. Sue thought Ms. Pearline possessed some magic. She had transformed a small living room, no larger than Sue's closet back home, into an oasis for "girls like us." Sue had witnessed, on the streets of Chicago and DC and in the halls of Congress, a versus nation. US versus the Vietcong. Hippies versus police. Teens versus parents. But somehow, with so little, Ms. Pearline blanked out race and war and anger, to paint over it all with pure acceptance and vibrant color.

The foul smell still held on until an arm began to stir beneath Sue. Then a leg kicked someone in the face.

"Ouch!"

And then everyone woke up to the smell.

"My Lord, who did that?"

"It was YOU!"

"No, it was not ME! It was YOU!"

"I know what your gas smells like, Mary—that was your gas!"

"I swear it wasn't me."

"Well, how do you know if you were asleep?"

"Uhh . . ."

"Ha! It was you!"

"Stop," Sue interrupted. "Stop it, girls. It's okay. It was me."

Sue's new nickname was Stankybooty, and it made her laugh every time.

• • •

The following day, as Sue strummed random tunes on her guitar, a pounding at the door scared them all silent.

"Open up!" yelled a forceful male voice. "Now!"

A man's voice in this place was not a welcome sound. After Michael had revealed himself as a poser, Sue realized most of them were selfish and pretentious, very much like her father. Women were altogether better.

"Girls," Ms. Pearline said before closing her robe tightly over her nightdress and long johns. "Go into my room and stay quiet."

They filed in before pressing their ears to the door in order to hear the conversation clearly.

"You're late with your money, Pearl," the man spat. He sounded drunk.

Sue could tell from his first, short sentence what type of man he was. A man who loved to take out misplaced aggressions on women. A bully of a sucker of a man. She couldn't see him, but she visualized him large-bellied with dirty hands. She hated him without knowing him. Then she turned her hatred inward.

A free spirit at heart, Sue never regretted anything. She saw the world as a fishbowl filled to the brim with choices, all leading to the same singular destiny. For that reason, it didn't matter which path a person chose to walk. She would still wind up occupying the space she should at the exact time she was supposed to. But she should've made Michael wear that condom. Men like this, men like Michael, and men like her father fathered children. She knew that when she let him refuse the condom that day. *It's too small*, he'd said, the fucking liar. And she'd been dumb enough to go along with it.

"I believe I paid you in full, Mr. Reese," Ms. Pearline replied slowly and deliberately. "Here's last week's receipt you signed as proof."

He laughed. "I know you paid me. I came for my tip."

"Pardon me?" she replied with the cunning of a woman who knows how to handle belligerent men with outsize egos. "What kind of tip are you looking for? I gave you all I have." Her voice had taken on a hint of teasing, like a Kenilworth wife asking for a bigger diamond ring.

"A tip for incentive," he said. "Not to tell the authorities that you're running a baby factory out of your apartment, that's what." His slurred speech made him hard to understand, but all four girls caught his threat loud and clear. "I hear the screams. I see the neighbors coming with blankets and little hats. I'm not stupid, Pearl. You treat me like an idiot."

Sue ran into people like this at her rallies and marches. They were usually on the other side, angry that hippies like her would dare wear what they wore and do what they did. She pitied those people. No one should be that mad about anything. She'd scurry to the front of the picket line, hang her guitar over her shoulder, and play for them. But it only made them angrier. Once, a man who sounded drunk like Mr. Reese threw his beer bottle at her guitar. There was still a dent in the soundboard near the pick guard. Glass shattered, nicking her thumb and pinkie finger. It bled like hell, but it didn't hurt at all. For the longest time, the wood smelled like blood and beer.

"I know you're not an idiot, Mr. Reese," said Ms. Pearline in an even softer, more feminine tone. "You're the smartest man around here." She giggled.

"Smart enough to see that rich guitar over there," Mr. Reese said cunningly. "My uncle plays, and that thing looks like it cost a pretty penny."

Ms. Pearline was quick. "That old thing? I got that from a Junior League thrift shop. See how it's all beat up and dented? Cost next to nothing."

Mr. Reese let out a joyful sound that only comes from a stroked ego that doesn't deserve stroking. Sue in no way pitied this man. Actually, she wanted to storm the living room and strangle him. But, in that moment, she recognized the danger of her presence. She wanted to ignore it, but it hit her like a brick between the eyes.

If she showed herself to anyone, even by accident, the whole thing could fall to pieces. Sue looked around her—Lillian tried to look unaffected, Mary came off as nervous as Ms. Pearline, and Missippi was adorable and curious even now. The last thing Sue ever wanted was to get any of these girls in trouble. She knew her being there made them more vulnerable. She gave off something she'd never been able to pinpoint. There was something in her posture or her way of speaking. Something in the way she walked or carried her guitar. She reeked of wealth without even trying. Everyone she met wanted to know what her father did because of it. And if that horrible man stormed through the door to find her there, who knows what he might've done to access that wealth.

Sue thought of Ms. Pearline. Two days ago she wouldn't have imagined that such a woman could exist in the world.

A woman willing to sacrifice everything, her whole life and youth, for a cause bigger than herself. Sue wanted to be that kind of woman, but she knew she wasn't. Sure, she marched and held up signs and stuck flowers in police helmets. That was something, she thought. Well, it wasn't nothing. But at night she curled into her plush bed and threw her day's clothes on the floor for her maid to pick up and wash the following day.

She was no activist. Not really. Ms. Pearline was what true sacrifice looked like.

• • •

Later that night, when everyone else was asleep, Sue found Missippi sitting on the windowsill, her round face glowing in the moonlight and her extra-large belly squished against the glass. Missippi looked like a brown Madonna painting. Haloed, young, and free of guilt. Who did this to this girl? Sue couldn't help thinking.

Sue, herself, chose sex. She'd made a decision to sleep with whoever she wanted and didn't care much what anyone thought about that. But she knew that sex could be awful and dirty and traumatizing. She thought of herself at Sippi's age. Sex wasn't something she really thought about back then. It had only come into her orbit her second year in high school.

"You awake, Sue?" Missippi whispered. "I see you peeking. Come on over."

Sue slowly lifted Lillian's or Mary's forearm from her thigh and eased her way up from the crowded bed to sit next to Missippi in the window.

"They stay out there all night long," Missippi said as she pointed to the young boys illuminated under the glow of a streetlamp. "I wish I knew what they was saying."

"I know," Sue said before nudging Missippi's arm. "Let's give them dialogue. Make up what they're saying from up here."

Missippi laughed. "I do that back home. I'm good at it!"

"Okay, let's go." Sue waited for one of the boys to make a move. As the one in the green shirt began to swing on the swing set, Sue began in a fake deep voice. "Hey, I'm Greg. Do I look like a Greg to you?"

Missippi picked it up without a hitch. "Yeah, brother. You look like a Greg to me. What I look like to you? How 'bout a George? I look like a George to you?"

"Sure do to me. Hey, George?"

"Yeah, Greg?"

"Why do we hang out here so late every single night?" Sue asked, still faking a deeper voice than her own. "We should really get some sleep."

"Sleep, Greg, psshhht. Sleep is for babies. We can

swing all night and jump on the monkey bars until the sun come up."

Missippi and Sue laughed so hard they almost woke up the others. They became friends without any effort whatsoever. It was an easy union. Immediate and easy.

A low growl emitted from Missippi's stomach, and she released an enormous fart that smelled like rotten meat. Sue wanted to gag at the smell, but she held it in, since she didn't want to embarrass Missippi.

"I can't control them anymore." Missippi hung her head. "I think somebody's squeezing something out from the inside."

"It's okay," Sue replied.

"I should've spoke up and told the other girls it was me the other night," Missippi told her quietly. "They call you Stanky, but it's me that's stanky. I'm sorry."

"It's really okay." Sue leaned in closer. "I don't mind one bit. You can blame your farts on me anytime you like."

Missippi smiled and stared at Sue for a long time. "Can I tell you something?"

"You can tell me anything in the whole world," Sue replied with a gentle grin.

Missippi looked down at her large stomach, and her face dropped. "You can't tell another soul, and if you do, I'll know, 'cause don't nobody else know."

Sue held up two fingers. "Scout's honor."

"My dead mama's brother did this to me," Missippi said, almost matter-of-fact. "I don't like talking about it or thinking about it. But if I got two of his little ones in my belly, will they come out wrong? Twisted up, I mean?"

Sue felt like she'd been run over by a truck. Flattened into the ground and sinking in deeper. Words escaped her. She didn't want to answer, but she knew she had to. She wiped her face clear of the terror she felt on the inside and forced the words out one by one.

"No, Sippi," she said before grabbing her in for an embrace. "Your babies will be perfect, just like you are."

Missippi pulled back to look Sue in the eyes and smile. "That's what my daddy calls me. Sippi."

IZELLA/OLA

24 Weeks & 6 Days

A little over three months had passed since Walter and Izella took Ola to Mrs. Mac's, and Ola was a brand-new gal. Even Walter was more himself, smiling and hugging Ola like they used to at the rec center. Izella, though, was more relieved than all of them put together.

She'd had the worry of the world on her little shoulders, and all the foolishness about keeping or not keeping babies was raising hive bumps in her forearms. Her fifteen-year-old self had flipped a coin in her mind and decided Mrs. Mac getting rid of the baby was the way to go, and thank the Lord she was right. Because if she wasn't right, she would've never forgiven herself. Not ever for the rest of her life, and she had a lot of life left to live. But that was neither here nor there. Mrs. Mac had done it.

After mixing up her smelly potion, Mrs. Mac had poured a whole bottle of Three Sixes elixir into the basin and given Ola a big bottle of syrup to take every morning for seven days. She told them that baby would be gone by midweek, but the whole bottle would help get her along to heaven. Izella noticed Ola cringe every time Mrs. Mac called the baby a *her* or a *she*, and Mrs. Mac had the sight enough to see it, too. Izella wanted to kick Mrs. Mac when she did it. She knew good and well it was done on purpose.

As soon as they left Mrs. Mac's house that night, Izella decided never to fix any more of her sister's problems. If she was going to be stupid, she was going to be stupid all on her own. No more help from her. No, ma'am, not ever.

"You feeling all right?" Izella asked Ola, noticing a slight spread in her sister's hips. "You got a shape."

Ola reached to the back of the closet and picked out a light green shift dress with flowers across the top. She was wearing a too-small girdle pulled all the way up to her bra. "I'm feeling better than ever, Babygal! Like the old me."

Izella felt a tiny bit of pride shoot through her body.

She'd done it. She'd sent everything back to the way it was supposed to be. Her sister was picking out dresses and letting down pin curls. No grown-folks' talk about having babies and picket fences and nonsense. Ola owed her big-time, Izella thought. If it wasn't for her, she'd be crawling around the bathroom floor in the yellow instead of twirling circles in the closet like a happy girl.

"You owe me." Izella couldn't help herself. She'd been handling Ola with kid gloves for months now, and she was due a thousand thank-yous for all she had done for her big sister. "You owe me big-time."

"Owe you?" Ola replied, shocked. "You didn't do nothing, Babygal. I would've thought to go to Mrs. Mac myself before too long."

"You ain't smart enough to do nothing like that!" Izella shot out of bed. "Besides, you didn't even know what Mrs. Mac was before I told you."

"Keep your voice down!" Ola said before rehanging the dress in the closet. "Evangelist might hear you."

"Don't you tell me to keep my voice down, you!" Izella said with the same disdain Mrs. Mac had when speaking to Ola. "I nearly ripped my hair out trying to get you and Walter out of the mess you made. And you tell me I ain't done nothing? That's it. I'm telling."

Izella walked to the bedroom door. She wasn't going

to tell Evangelist on Ola. She would never do such a thing, but she wanted to scare her sister straight. Share in some of the pain of being overlooked and not recognized for all she'd done.

Ola grabbed Izella's arm. "Okay, okay. You did it all, and I'm so grateful."

Izella folded her arms, knowing she must look like a spoiled, stubborn child, but she didn't care. "What else?"

"You told me about Mrs. Mac."

"What else?"

"You cleaned up after me."

"What else?"

"You covered for me, too."

"What else?"

"What else you want?" Ola asked, frustrated.

"I want you to never call me Babygal ever again," Izella told her. "Ever!"

"Fine."

• • •

Even though Evangelist's breakfast prayer was extra long, Izella and Ola didn't peek at each other once. Izella was mad because Ola was such an ungrateful hag, and Ola was mad that Izella was such a self-righteous brat.

Still, when Ola cleared her plate for the first time in weeks, joy went through Izella's body.

"These cheese grits are delicious, Evangelist," Ola said with a mouthful. "Better than any I ever had."

"They need to be," Evangelist replied. "I'd been cooking them every morning for Missippi. I just about have them perfect now."

"How she doing?" asked Izella, knowing the simple question could launch Evangelist into an hour-long rant. That was okay, though. The silence at the tiny table needed filling.

"I miss that ole gal," Evangelist said, shaking her head. "I never thought I would. But I miss her."

Ola and Izella looked at each other, both scared something awful had happened.

"Where she go?" they asked together.

"A few weeks ago, her papa sent her away to have her baby," Evangelist said before stuffing a butter biscuit in her mouth. "Gal grew on me back when I was seeing about her. Such a sad soul, no mama and barely no papa. Every time I went by to drop off grits, she begged me to come on in and show her how to be a girl. Poor thing was all covered up in dirt and car oil when I first started going over there. She didn't even know how to hold a mop, but after I showed her, she cleaned that little house top to bottom. Almost as good as you two girls."

"They let girls that young have they babies?" asked Ola. Izella kicked her hard under the table. "Ouch!"

"They really don't have much of a choice now, do they?" Evangelist asked with a touch of anger. "Why you care? You better not come here talking about you having no baby."

Ola looked at her plate.

"Fig tree is about near overloaded." Izella jumped in reflexively to cover for her sister. She couldn't help it. It was a knee-jerk reaction—helping stupid Ola not get in trouble. "We might need to set up a stand out front again this year and sell by the pound. We made a pretty penny last year, remember?"

"I saw them out there yesterday," Evangelist replied before taking a hefty bite of bacon. "Still golf-ball-sized and hard green, I'd say. Hey, I was thinking of making Mr. Melvin and the boys some preserves, and catching the bus over to Tuskegee. What y'all think?"

"That's a nice idea," said Izella, happy Evangelist had moved on from Missippi and babies and other nonsense. "I liked them a lot."

"Me too," Ola added, mouth overflowing. "He was funny, Flossie." Ola teased her mother.

The two girls laughed. Evangelist never looked or acted like a Flossie. Not until she was in the same room with Mr. Melvin, that is.

"Stop that now," said Evangelist with a small, shy, unfamiliar smile. "He's a friend."

"A friend you want to take homemade fig preserves all the way to Tuskegee for?" asked Ola.

"No, no," said Izella. "A friend you let call you Flossie."

They chuckled again.

"Y'all need to stay out of grown-folks' business." Evangelist stood from the table and went to the counter, turning her back to the girls.

Izella also stood and began gathering utensils from the table. "It's okay," she said. "We liked Mr. Melvin. Ain't that right, Ola?"

"Yep. We hear y'all talking on the phone all times of night like you slick," Ola said. "He'll make as good a daddy as any other, I'd say."

Evangelist dropped the dishes in the sink with a crash. "Girls." She turned back around to face her daughters. "No soul on earth could ever replace your daddy, you hear?"

"Yes, ma'am," they said together.

"We forgot our manners," added Izella.

"Yes, you did," Evangelist assured them.

As they cleared the breakfast table, they heard a female voice humming "Oh Happy Day" up the walkway.

"You expecting somebody, Evangelist?" asked Ola.

Evangelist shrugged. "Not until later on. Must be a

church member come to say hi. Y'all girls finish up in here while I let them in."

Ola and Izella did as they were told and took to the dishes—Ola sudsing them up and Izella drying. Izella kicked Ola square in the bottom.

"Don't hit me, you cow!" Ola hollered out. "That hurt."

"I didn't hit you."

"Who did, then? A ghost?" Ola dropped her dish and went to pinch Izella's side, but Izella was too quick.

"Maybe it was a ghost," Izella replied, jumping around the kitchen to avoid being pinched. "'Cause it wasn't me."

"You must really think I'm stupid, don't you?"

"Nobody's stupid in this kitchen," announced a hauntingly familiar voice. "Two of my favorite gals."

"Look who it is!" Evangelist said with pure joy in her voice. "It's a miracle happening right here in Valdosta, Georgia. I can't believe my own eyes."

As Mrs. Mac crossed into their kitchen, Izella's and Ola's jaws dropped open in shock. She looked like an entirely different woman. Gray hair flowing down her back like a spring, skin alive and glowing, back straight, and eyes alive and less grayed over. She looked thirty years younger than she had the night before. But the sight of her terrified them. "Haven't seen y'all gals in a minute. Where you two been?"

Evangelist continued swooning over Mrs. Mac's appearance and completely missed the fact that her daughters hadn't taken her bread in months. "How is this possible? God himself must've picked you up out that bed. You look like a spry young thing!"

Mrs. Mac placed her spindly fingers on Evangelist's shoulder and smiled. Izella and Ola both wanted to flick her fingers off their mother. Witchcraft brought her back like this. Toiling and tinkering with young lives had given her a new lease on hers. She was trouble, they wanted to tell Evangelist. But they just stayed quiet and watched.

"It was your homemade bread that brought me back this side of heaven, child," Mrs. Mac said to Evangelist. "So I come to bring you something I made for a change."

The girls gasped as Mrs. Mac pulled the hand-carved ship Ola had stepped on a few months earlier from her satchel and handed it to Evangelist. Evangelist held it in her hands in awe.

"You made this yourself?" Evangelist asked with tears in her eyes. "I never seen anything like it."

"Took years," Mrs. Mac said, nodding. "Once a girl stepped on it, and I thought she'd cracked it in two." She winked at Ola, and Ola cringed in return. "But it survived. Somebody need to hold on to it after I'm dead and gone. Ain't nobody good as you. Probably be worth real money if you keep it away from clumsy little girls who don't watch where they stepping."

Evangelist held it to her chest. "I'll keep it in the top drawer with my wedding rings, where nobody goes but me. I'll be right back."

As Evangelist turned the corner, Mrs. Mac eyeballed Ola skeptically. "You a little liar, gal. A filthy little lying little girl."

Izella's instinct kicked in. "You don't talk to my sister like that."

Mrs. Mac laughed a horrible cackle. "Defending her now, you are? Well, that's nice. Watch her ruin your promise like she done already ruined her own."

"You don't know what you talking about," Izella snapped. "We going on to live good lives. We ain't doing nothing else stupid. Right, Ola?"

Izella noticed Ola didn't answer. Instead, she stared at Mrs. Mac, who stared right back at her knowingly. Izella felt like a third wheel. An intruder butting into a conversation she wasn't welcome in. In that moment, she felt young and naive. She hated feeling that way, so she pushed that aside and exchanged it for anger.

"Ola ain't no fool!" Izella told Mrs. Mac, who was showing a mouth full of old teeth. "She might was before, but she ain't no more."

But still, they both stayed silent and stared at each other without blinking. Then Evangelist appeared in the doorway, and the moment passed.

"I can't thank you enough, Mrs. Mac," she said. "You wouldn't believe how few folks think to thank me, let alone bring me things. And I can't get over how good you looking. Why don't I fix you a glass of sweet tea and you tell me about the fountain of youth you found."

Mrs. Mac tilted her head and grinned. "Oh, no, thank you. I need to get on back home," she said before resting her gaze on Ola again. "Don't worry, though. I'll be back to check on what's what."

"Anytime," Evangelist said. "You're welcome any-time."

She was not welcome, Izella and Ola thought.

• • •

For the next few days, Ola and Izella kept turning over Mrs. Mac's strange visit. Talking and fussing over it.

"That old fool," said Ola. "She's just talking. Ain't no truth in her."

"Ola!" Izella replied, frustrated. "You saw what she can do. The woman's touched."

"Touched by demons and not much else," Ola said while clipping her nails and pretending not to give a care.

"I'll tell you one thing. I'm not taking her another bite of bread ever again. She can curl up in that bed and crumble for all I care."

Izella couldn't understand it. They'd been sitting around the same table. Watching and listening to the same things that night. Walter, Ola, and she had seen a woman send a baby on to heaven like a poof! Gone! And stupid Ola still doubted her.

Izella used to like Mrs. Mac. Never love. She was too smart to love such a potent woman. Loving Mrs. Mac would be like loving a vial of deadly poison. Petting it and sipping on it until it killed you. Never love, not even once. But she respected Mrs. Mac for what she was. Stupid, stupid, stupid Ola, she thought. Would she ever not be this stupid?

Izella sat back on their bed and watched her older sister get dressed and ready for the day. It was a strong Valdosta Friday—rumbling clouds and mean, biting rain. Izella would wear overalls in such weather, knee-scraped ones that nobody cared whether they got ripped or scuffed. But she watched as stupid, stupid Ola hummed through her pretty closet in her girdle, pulling out pastel skirts and button-down tops. Izella knew she would come home mad and muddy like always.

One time, a few months ago in the spring, Ola had

to throw out a fresh pair of white stockings. On a day much like this one, she'd been standing in the same spot that morning. Picking out the stupidest possible outfit to wear on such a rainy day. Izella told her not to wear them. She'd warned her not to do what she was about to do, but no, no, no. Ola knew what she wanted to wear. Not too long after they left the house, a bus splattered a full puddle onto her pretty white legs. She came home covered in muck and scrubbed those stockings for hours, but it was no use. Stupid Ola had to throw them out. Just like she had to throw out her baby a few months ago.

Izella tried not to hate her sister. But it was getting harder.

Evangelist knocked on their bedroom door. "Girls," she said in a voice of exuberance. "We riding up to see Mr. Melvin tomorrow! So we need to get all of our deliveries out the way today. Double Mrs. Mac's bread. And y'all need to eat a banana and some figs on the walk. No time for breakfast. I'm heading on out!"

Izella heard Evangelist whistling her way down the hall. She whistled louder and stronger than anybody in Valdosta, especially when she was happy.

"I think she really likes that man," Ola started. "Old Mr. Melvin."

"Who *don't* like that man?"

Ola rolled her eyes. "He was kinda funny, I guess."

"You guess?" Izella wanted to smack some sense into her. "He gave you his most prized possession! And you guess?"

"Oh," Ola said before stepping into another fresh pair of white stockings on a muddy, rainy day. "You believe that story? Only a baby would believe that. He made it up. Pennies don't flip up to heaven and come back down hours later burnt up. He probably ran over and over that thing with a tractor, and scorched it with a match. You believe anything you told, girl."

Izella could hardly breathe. The last thing she wanted was to actually call her sister stupid to her face, but she felt the word rising up inside her. Why couldn't Ola ever see the obvious things? The penny wasn't important. It was the story that mattered. The wisdom of heeding warnings from those who'd touched the stove, so you didn't have to. It was not fair at all. Being the younger sister to a stupid was not fair!

"Where is it?" Izella forced each words out of her mouth slowly and deliberately so as not to scream them at her.

"Where is what?"

"You know what!"

"Oh." Ola pointed at her jewelry box. "I put that old

dirty penny in the top. You better be glad I didn't spend it."

Izella went to grab it, and she noticed her hand was shaking. She was losing control of herself and her emotions. She needed to get away from Ola before she said or did something she couldn't take back. Izella grabbed the penny and took off running through the kitchen.

"Where you going, cow?" Ola yelled after her.

"To take Mrs. Mac her bread," Izella yelled back.

"Good! Go by yourself, then," said Ola. "I'm going to the rec center! And put my penny back where you found it when you get home!"

• • •

The short walk to Mrs. Mac's house was a terrifying thing.

Soon as she stepped out the back door, she happened upon a long black snake racing across her yard. He was shiny like a greased-up tire. And Izella would swear he stopped at the hedge, stood straight up, looked her dead in the eye, and smiled. When she blinked one good time, he was gone on. She hurried along to jump Mr. Turner's back fence to find his son, Stanley, sipping on white lightning.

She tried to pretend she hadn't seen him. They shared a birthday, she and Stanley. He was exactly a year to the day older than her, and every year Evangelist made her knock on his door to wish him a happy birthday. Izella never did like Stanley. He never helped his mama with groceries. Izella watched him sit and sip as his mama dragged a head of peaches up the sidewalk. And, too, he smelled like his daddy—liquor and sweat. She didn't want to speak to him, but he hollered out to her.

"Hey!" he said, holding up a flask. "Want some?"

Another stupid, Izella thought. Why was everybody around her so stupid?

"No, thank you, Stanley," she said. "I'm in a hurry."

"Suit yourself," he said before lounging back. "You don't know what you're missing."

Something cracked inside her body. A twig broke open her angry floodgates, and she lost control. "What I'm missing, Stanley?" she started, fuming. "What I'm missing? You mean sitting in the dirt all day drunker than Cooter Brown? Is that what I'm missing? You mean sweating stink, too? And letting your poor mama all but wipe your tail, huh? Oh, and stumbling to walk a straight line? If that's what I'm missing, stupid, stupid Stanley Turner, then I'll keep right on missing it."

Stanley stared off in the distance, never making eye contact with Izella. He looked sad and slumped like a walrus. She was immediately sorry for going off like that. He didn't deserve it. Well, even if he did deserve it, it hadn't been for her to say.

"You see that black racer snake going across a minute ago?" he asked without acknowledging her rant whatsoever.

"I saw," she replied before sitting down next to him on his stoop. "Thought I was the only one who had."

Stanley, glassy-eyed and slurring, looked her directly in the eyes without blinking and said, "Racers don't usually mean no harm. They in after gopher rats and rabbits. Once, I saw one take on an opossum, and get bit up so he passed on, but not before eating up that opossum." Stanley laughed to himself at the memory and took another sip. "But when they stand up on the tip-tails and look at you, you got some bad things coming. Bad, bad things coming." He then took a long, slow drag from his flask. "You sure you don't want a little help getting through it?"

"I'm sure," Izella said before reaching into her bag and pulling out one of the two loaves of bread. "Have a loaf to soak some of that stuff up."

"See you later on." Stanley took it, smiled, and lifted his flask. "And a happy early birthday to you."

The rest of the walk to Mrs. Mac's took on the color gray. Gray mad skies opened up to drop a drench of rain onto Valdosta. Two gray cats trying to find shelter were nearly hit by a car. And the car that almost hit them was pewter gray. Izella ran for Mrs. Mac's front porch, where it was dry, and there the woman sat, creaking back and forth on the swing.

"Too wet to go straight back home, child," Mrs. Mac said in a low voice with no anger. She spoke to Izella differently than she spoke to Ola. She liked her—that much was obvious. "Don't just drop off the loaf and leave. Stay awhile."

Mrs. Mac got up from the swing and opened the screen door.

"You fixed it," Izella said, amazed that the door had all three hinges and screws in place. "How?"

"Not me, child," said Mrs. Mac, grinning. "I'll fix you some tea."

Drenched, Izella followed her inside the home. She shouldn't have, but she did.

It was altogether different in the light of day. Clean, organized, and with everything in its place, it looked like a museum of artifacts. Masks framed the walls, some carved from oak and others from stone. The couch that had been covered was now bare. Its wooden legs intricate with cherubs, and the gold-threaded trim stitched with detail and designs. Izella had never seen anything like it. But the most dramatic piece, by far, was the mahogany curio of men.

Izella stood in front of it and stared. "What is it?" she asked.

"My collection," said Mrs. Mac without looking up from making the tea. "I'd always wanted fifty. But forty-nine was all I got to."

Izella stepped back to look over the entire collection. They had personality, each of them, like they were alive or had been once. One wore a tilted fedora, another dark sunglasses, and another had thick sideburns and an inch-high Afro.

"Did you kill them all?"

Mrs. Mac laughed outright before walking over with two cups of tea. She handed one to Izella, but Izella just looked in it skeptically.

"You think I'm going to kill you, child?" Mrs. Mac asked, smiling through all of her teeth and setting the cup down on the coffee table. "No, I didn't kill them. But I didn't let them live, either."

Izella sat across from Mrs. Mac to get a good view of who she was dealing with. A loud, horrible crash of thunder shook the teacup, and Mrs. Mac grinned even wider. "Somebody's mad as hell up there today," she said.

"Who are they?" Izella asked. "The men."

"They all got thrown in"—Mrs. Mac motioned

toward the basin she'd used to mix Ola's baby's potion—"that washbasin over there."

Izella remembered the moment Mrs. Mac had rubbed her hands together and said, *This baby needs to be thrown into the wash.* Then she'd got rid of Ola's baby girl.

"What does it mean?"

"It means," Mrs. Mac started. "You haven't touched your tea. It's getting cold."

Mrs. Mac took a slurp of her own tea and looked over the cup at her.

"Who are they?"

"You know who they are, child," she spat. "Don't act stupid like that sister of yours. You ain't never been no fool. Don't waste your mind acting like one."

"The baby was a boy," Izella said almost to herself. "Not a girl. They all were—boys."

Mrs. Mac was right. Izella knew who they were. Every single one of them. She knew that night when she'd first seen them. She just didn't want to accept that what she thought was the truth. These were all the babies that'd been thrown into the washbasin. Or what they would've become if they hadn't been. Izella jumped up and kicked over her tea.

Mrs. Mac laughed again. "You a spitfire," she said. "I'll give you that much."

"You're a witch!"

"I ain't no witch, child," she said without as much as a hint of anger. "I'm just an old cripple lady trapped in a house, waiting on one stupid girl and one smart girl to bring me my bread. I'll tell you what, though. That sister is taking you down with her. Soon, too."

"What does that mean?" Izella asked, unable to resist the urge to scream at this horrible woman's teeth. "How will my sister take me down with her? You fixed it! You changed it!"

Mrs. Mac turned up her teacup and then set it down on the table. "I did my part, child. But I didn't near fix it. Your stupid sister . . ." She shook her head. "Check her bottom drawer when you get home."

Mrs. Mac stood and stopped in front of her curio of men. Anger crept into her face, and her smile sunk into a dangerous glare. She stared at Izella, who, for the first time, felt real terror at the sight of her.

"I did my part! Go tell that gal to get me my fifty!"

• • •

Izella took the long way home—sidewalks only. She didn't want to risk seeing the Turner boy or any snakes. The sky had cleared up, and her world turned back blue. She burst through the door to find her mother sitting on the couch. But Evangelist never sat and did nothing. Something was going on.

"What's wrong, Evangelist?" Izella asked. Her mother must've found whatever was in the bottom drawer. There was no other explanation for it. Sitting in silence was torture for a busybody like her mother who was always doing something with her hands. Even when resting, she knitted or crocheted or scrubbed something. Sometimes Izella thought she saw Evangelist make a spill just so she could have a reason to clean. To Izella's surprise, Evangelist smiled.

"Nothing's wrong, Babygal," her mother said. "Where's your sister?"

"She's at the rec center." Izella told the truth. It felt good to tell the truth for a change, even if it wasn't the whole one. "She'll be home before the streetlights."

"I wanted to tell y'all when you was together, but I can't wait much longer. I feel like I might burst if I don't say it out loud, and you always had a way with listening." Izella knew her rants well, but this one seemed altogether different. "You promise to act like you surprised when I tell you and your sister together?"

Izella nodded.

"It's Mr. Melvin," Evangelist said, hiding her wide smile behind her hands. "He asked me for my hand."

It was the right thing, Izella thought. Mr. Melvin, the gentleman storyteller, was built from the floor up to be Evangelist's husband. He could handle her like no one else Izella had seen—with care but also with strength.

Evangelist, with all of her giving, was a master at shutting people down. Instinctively, she knew just the right thing to say to make another person hang their head and shut their mouth. Izella and Ola were trained from birth to do what their mother wanted, strategically avoiding her wrath, but outsiders could be flattened by Evangelist's words. Men especially were susceptible to her judgmental tongue.

Once, Izella had witnessed Evangelist turn down a proposal outright from a man who was still legally married. He was on one knee when she called him a male harlot and dismissed him from her presence in Jesus's name. It'd seemed harsh, but it was the absolute truth. He'd slept with all of Valdosta before that proposal. That was another thing about Evangelist. She told the truth, even if it hurt.

Now here she was. Gushing like Ola over a man wise enough to handle a strong woman's strength. Izella felt happy for her.

"That's wonderful, Mama." She grabbed both of her mother's hands and kissed them.

The smile on her mama's face was the sweetest thing

Izella could remember. Evangelist just sat in her chair grinning. No snap peas set in her lap. No laundry to tend. Or daughters to pray for. Finally free of things to do and people to see. Actually, there probably were things to do, but she didn't seem to care. She was in love. Evangelist had gotten a turn to be in love herself, Izella thought. After all the folks to feed and clean up after. It was her turn. And nobody deserved a turn more than Prophetess/Evangelist Flossie Murphy.

"Go on and clean up for dinner now," Evangelist said, smiling into the hardwoods. "And don't forgot to act surprised."

Izella scuffled on to the bathroom. She was covered in filth from the muddy day and needed a good scrubbing. After throwing cold water on her face, she ran herself a warm tub bath and thought of finding her mama smiling at the end of that awful day. From fighting with stupid Ola at sunrise to the shiny racer snake at noonday. That drunken Turner boy when the sun heated up Valdosta to the sky opening up gray on the way to Mrs. Mac's creaky porch swing.

And then it hit her.

"The bottom drawer," she said to herself, unable to believe she'd let it slip her crowded mind.

She abandoned the running bath and took off for her

room down the hall. She wouldn't be that long. Check the drawer and come on back in for a warm, well-deserved sit-down in the tub.

Izella opened the drawer to find nothing out of the ordinary. Just stupid Ola's stupid pastel panties and girdles. When she dug around a bit, she felt a solid piece of something wrapped up in a tube sock. She lifted it out and held it in her hands.

It all made sense when she pinched the toe of the sock and pulled it off the solid piece of something. Ola was a lying girl and a stupid one. Izella held on to the untouched bottle of Mrs. Mac's elixir so tightly that she thought her grasp might shatter it in her hands. Not even a sip was missing from the bottle. It was so full that the liquid hit the lip of the rim. After all of that. Everything she'd gone through to get her sister out of the mess she was in. She didn't have the decency to do her tiny part and drink the stuff.

Izella didn't cry. It wasn't her way. But she sat there long enough to overflow the tiny bathroom with warm tub water.

• • •

Izella played sick for the rest of the night and woke up before the sun to watch Ola sleep. A thin ray of light lit up her face. Izella noticed it, clear as day, a tiny heartbeat pumping in the side of her neck. She wanted to pinch it off like a mosquito. Or swat it like a housefly. But it pumped on—pump, pump, pump.

Izella glanced at the two small bags on their bedroom floor packed for Tuskegee. The bus would leave early that morning. She didn't want to go anymore. More than anything, she wanted to curl up and sleep until the world made a little sense like it had before. Before Evangelist had Mr. Melvin. Before Ola had Walter and a baby boy she didn't want to get rid of. Before she was all alone with nobody. Ola was a stupid girl, but Izella knew she herself was a selfish girl.

The bottom drawer that held the solution to all of her problems was a few feet away. She went to sit in front of it.

"Time to get ready, girls!" Evangelist yelled out cheerfully. "Don't want that bus taking off without us in it."

Izella quickly opened the drawer, pulled out the sock, and popped up from the floor before Ola saw what was what. She tucked the elixir into the side pocket of her bag, and then Ola began to stir.

"She sounds like a schoolgirl," Ola muttered in her early-morning voice. "You was sleep when I got in last night. How you feel about this Mr. Melvin business?"

Izella shrugged as she watched stupid Ola flick the

crusty coal from her eye and yawn dramatically. She was scared to speak; even a nicety like *good morning* might bring all of the anger out her mouth. So she glued her lips together.

"You ain't got to answer, then," said Ola before swinging her legs around and dangling them off the side of the bed. "I don't like it one bit. I give it a month."

Izella nipped the tip of her tongue with her teeth to keep herself quiet.

"Suit yourself." Ola kept right on talking. "Since you not saying nothing, I'll go ahead and tell you that Walter's been so happy lately—smiling and grinning like he used to. We kissed and hugged up at the rec center yesterday. It really did feel like before he went off to war. He's got a whole new outlook. I do, too. Oh! And I keep seeing the number three around town everywhere I go. The number three bus go by and then three kids skipping down the sidewalk and then I pass three flowers grouped together. I think that mean we gone have three little ones before too long."

Izella tasted salty blood in her mouth and smelled it, too. It smelled like fresh iron from the mines. She bit down harder, but it was no use. A geyser was about to break on the inside. A gushing of mad. A full explosion building and building up from the white soles of her feet.

She had never been so full of hell in all of her life. The devil himself stirred in her bones, and she could kill stupid, stupid Ola right there if she released him.

"Come on, girls!" Evangelist said. "Y'all got fifteen minutes to walk out the door. I made muffins for breakfast. Grab one and we need to go."

Ola passed Izella as if nothing was wrong. "Dibs on the bathroom." And she disappeared through the door.

Izella forced breath through her body and got dressed in any old thing.

• • •

"You haven't touched your muffin, Babygal," Evangelist said on the bus ride to Tuskegee. "It was good, wasn't it, Ola?"

"It was!" said Ola. "Best muffin I've had in a long while."

Evangelist chuckled. "Ola, you been really enjoying my food lately. Cleaning your plate like I never seen you do."

"You got a way with it, Evangelist," Ola complimented her. "I'll take yours if you not gonna eat it, Izella."

It's not Ola at all, Izella thought. That hungry little boy inside is cleaning her plate for her. Greedy monster, stealing food and sisters. Izella handed her muffin to the little boy inside her big sister. As if he hadn't taken everything else from her, now here he was taking her muffin.

Sure she didn't want it, but still. Take, take, take, little heathen, take, take, take.

They zoomed past the sign saying they were 157 miles away from Tuskegee. Smooth roads and a straight shot, Evangelist had told them. Easy road there, easy road back. It was the opposite of an easy ride.

Ola kept pestering Izella—blowing in her ears and pulling at her plats. She had no idea what a bear she was poking. Stupid, stupid girl. When they reached the Alabama Dixie sign, Izella had had enough.

Izella glared at Ola with all the evil she could find inside her. "Don't you touch me ever again, you!" She'd unintentionally stolen Mrs. Mac's *you*, and it shook Ola to the deep core.

"Why you mad, Babygal?" Ola asked, stunned. "What I do to you?"

Izella got up from her seat and headed to the way back of the bus.

"Where y'all going?" Evangelist asked. "We ain't got but a couple hours left to ride."

Instead of answering, Izella motioned Ola to join her in the back.

"We'll be right back, Evangelist," Ola told her mother. "Just going to talk a minute."

Izella plopped down in the window seat and crossed

her arms as she glared hatred onto her sister. Ola cautiously sat next to her, watching Izella's hands like she might get smacked. Finally, Izella thought. Stupid girl paying attention to something other than her own prissy tail.

"You look lightning-hot mad, Babygal."

"I told you, stupid girl! Don't call me Babygal!" Izella accidentally screamed it.

"What on earth is happening back there, girls?" Evangelist hollered over the seats. "Don't make me come back there and get y'all."

Izella bit blood from her tongue again while Ola apologized for the outburst. It felt backward, older sister apologizing for younger sister.

"I'm sorry, Izella. Tell me what's what, because I ain't never seen you look this mad ever. You smoking."

Izella released her bloody tongue from her teeth. She thought of the black racer snake. This is what he must feel like all the time—forking teeth through tongue like he does. She wondered had he ever bitten his by mistake. Then, slowly and deliberately, she lifted the sock from the side pocket of her bag and shoved it into Ola's hands.

It was a flood of knowing, washing the stupid off Ola. Sparks clicked in her eyes, and it all began to make sense the same way it had the day before when Izella found the full bottle. Now everyone knew where everyone stood. It should've been a freeing moment, a clarifying moment, but it was worse than not knowing anything. The simplicity of sister/sister had passed, and now an ocean of mean, shark-filled water stood between them. There was no going back after that. No *sorry* strong enough to cross that large a body of water.

Tears filled Ola's big eyes. She looked like a cherub in a picture. "I couldn't," Ola said before sobbing quietly into her own hands. "A girl? I couldn't. I named her Madeline. Isn't that beautiful?"

Izella felt her top lip twitch with disgust. Tears were no match for the shit her sister had put her through over the last few months. "Madeline?" She laughed a cackle very much like Mrs. Mac's. "He is not a girl. Mrs. Mac told me yesterday. You having a greedy little boy to eat you out of house and home. No! Eat Evangelist out of house and home, because you ain't got nowhere else to go, stupid!"

Ola looked up at Izella, still in tears but no longer sad ones. Now they were angry, dangerous tears. "What do you mean? Not a girl. I always knew she was a girl, always. When she talks to me, she's a girl. A dainty one to boot."

"She lied to you, stupid!"

"Stop. Calling. Me. Stupid. Right. Now."

"What are you going to do?" Izella balled her fists,

almost wanting to fight some of her aggression out. A good swing over the head would probably make her feel a whole lot better. She hated her stupid sister. True, pure, untouched hatred without a doubt. "You'd never really do anything to me, you stupid girl."

Ola reeled back like a slingshot and smacked Izella clean across her face. It was a slap placed perfectly on the fleshiest part of the cheek. And even though Izella half expected it, she was utterly shocked by it. Maybe even a bit proud of her sister for not being such a pastel prissy princess. If she had guessed, she'd have thought Ola's slap would be a puny dud that stung a little like a switch. But it damn well hurt. When Izella regained her bearings, she pounced like a cheetah.

First, they rolled onto the rubbery tread of the bus aisle. Izella got in a punch here and there, but she couldn't get a square enough shot at Ola's stomach. That's where she really wanted to clobber her one. Right on that hungry little monster boy's head. When Ola realized where she was trying to hit, she went for Izella's throat.

Izella had never been squeezed around the neck before. Her legs went limp, and her hands floated to Ola's forearms. Her entire body began to panic like it was underwater. She tried to speak, but she could only whisper. Ola's thumbs were crushing something at the front of her neck near the Adam's apple. Her sister was squeezing the life from her.

She saw her mother standing over Ola. She was fuzzy at the edges, like a ghost, and there was distress all over her face. A few strange people surrounded Ola and pulled on her. They were all fuzzy, too, and only getting fuzzier. Pulling and pulling, but there was no use. Ola's eyes were black and fixed on Izella's. She shouldn't have tried to punch her in the stomach, Izella thought. She'd gone too far. And maybe she shouldn't have tried to make her get rid of her baby, too. She was selfish. Selfish and maybe a little bit stupid herself. The bus driver jerked the bus to the right, and Ola lost her grip. And then everything went black.

•••

Izella opened her eyes, and the people were no longer fuzzy. She no longer felt angry. She only felt sorry. Ola had squeezed the devil out of her.

"Oh, thank God," said Evangelist. "Babygal, I thought I'd lost you. What's wrong with you, Ola? The devil got a hold to you."

Izella looked back at Ola, sitting in the last row of the bus with her head in her hands. "You okay, Ola?" Izella asked through her squeezed-up throat.

Ola looked back at her sister and smiled the smallest possible smile. "I'm good. You?"

"I think somebody tried to choke me."

"I'm sorry," Ola said with tears in her eyes. "I don't know what came over me."

"I'm sorry, too," Izella whispered through her dry throat. "I came over you."

"You ain't got a thing to be sorry for, Babygal," Evangelist said, glaring at Ola. "Your older sister is the one need to be sorry."

Izella touched her mother's face. "Mama," she said, shocking Evangelist by calling her that. "Trust me when I say I deserved it."

Evangelist's eyes twitched with confusion. "Y'all girls trying to kill me. I swear it."

Izella sat up straight with the help of strangers. Someone handed her a thermos of water with ice, and she drank it all the way empty. "How far are we from Tuskegee?"

The bus driver yelled out, "Two exits away now."

Izella rose to her feet and sat down in the nearest empty seat. "My mama's about to get proposed to. You ready, Evangelist?"

Evangelist laid her heavy head in her youngest daughter's lap.

"If you ain't, you better get ready."

The bus rolled on for about fifteen more minutes and then came to a halt in its terminal. "We all made it alive, thank the Lord," said the driver as everyone shuffled toward the door. "Late, but alive. Good night to you all."

Evangelist was the third to last off the bus, and Izella watched as she handed the driver a four-pack of muffins from her bag as a thank-you. Izella followed closely behind and nodded to him as she stepped down. Ola was last off. By the time she finally made her way down the three steps, the terminal had cleared of all but Izella and Evangelist. They waited on the warm concrete. It was late, damp, and dark out with hundreds of large, batty bugs fighting for the fluorescent light.

In the light, Ola looked heaps worse than Izella felt. Like three-times-rolled-over hell. Her hair had fallen and frizzed from her flood of tears, and her lipstick had smeared into a swipe across the bottom half of her face. Her nose-blown dress had wrinkled from being used multiple times as a tissue. Ola was an altogether mess.

Izella looked to Evangelist, expecting a lecture from her about strangling and nearly killing her little sister, but if Evangelist felt judgment for her oldest, she didn't show it. Instead, she raked her fingers through Ola's hair.

"What are we going to do with you, child?" she said

before holding out her arm for a half hug and holding out the other one for Izella. "Y'all really trying to kill me, I swear it."

"Who's that trio of beautiful ladies over there?" Mr. Melvin's slow, kind voice hollered from an old-model blue truck in the lot. "A man would be mighty lucky to hold time with those lovely ladies."

Izella and Evangelist grinned, while Ola looked like she might tilt over. The three of them gathered their things and headed for the truck. Evangelist stopped halfway there. She seemed nervous and hesitant to close the space between her and Mr. Melvin.

"Just one moment, Mr. Melvin," she told him through an unfamiliar shaky voice. She turned around to face both of her daughters. "Is this right? Me and Mr. Melvin? Y'all would tell me if I'm wrong. I need y'all girls to be all right. Are y'all all right with this? If not, I swear I'll get right back on the next bus blazing."

"Evangelist," Ola started with the authority of a firstborn child. No stupid at all. Wisdom, strength, and knowing. "Do you love him?"

"What?"

Ola grabbed Evangelist by the shoulders and steadied her gaze. "Look at me. Do you love him?"

"I do."

“Does he love you?”

“He does.”

“Well, good,” Ola said as she released her mother’s shoulders. “You deserve joy more than anybody I know, except maybe Izella. You give up everything for everybody. Go get your joy, Mama.” Ola pointed to Mr. Melvin, who’d made his way out of the truck and to the concrete, where he knelt on one knee. “Joy’s waiting for you right over there.”

Mr. Melvin smiled and said, “Hurry on up, girls. I doubt I’ll make it up off this ground if you don’t come on here.”

• • •

Mr. Melvin lived in a sweet little green house that smelled like jowl bacon. A fresh pitcher of sweet tea sat sweating on the kitchen table, and the flowery tablecloth still had price tags on it. It was creased into squares like it had just been taken out of its packaging. He’d recently bought it, probably for them. Izella smiled at his effort, while Ola didn’t notice it at all.

He had a hard time getting through the door on his own legs. Izella knew many men like that back in Valdosta. Refusing, likely out of pride, to put in a wheelchair ramp. She didn’t like those kinds of men, too proud to acknowledge obvious shortcomings. But Mr. Melvin did it with a determined smile, like a child trying to prove he could walk without help from his mother. Mr. Melvin was adorable, Izella thought. And she'd never known a man that old to be adorable.

"I made too-sweet sweet tea." He lowered himself down to the table like he'd just run for miles and miles. "Y'all gone have to pour your own, though. My body's about done for the evening."

Evangelist waited in the doorway, watching her future husband sitting, out of breath and tired. She would have to help him every day, Izella realized. In and out of the tub, to the bathroom sink—she may even have to wipe his tail. For any other woman, this would've been a horrible realization. But for Evangelist, it was pure bliss. She was a woman who needed to be needed, and if she wasn't, she'd rock herself to death in her rocking chair.

"What's your last name, Mr. Melvin?" Izella asked. It had suddenly occurred to her that her mother would have to change her name to something she didn't know. "You'll be Evangelist Flossie something else soon."

"I'm Melvin Lesley Brooks the Third." He bowed. "Pleased to officially meet you ladies."

"Do you have siblings?" Izella took the empty seat next to him.

Mr. Melvin laughed. "Oh, I'd almost forgotten. You're

a curious one." Evangelist tried to interrupt, but he held his hand up. "The curious ones touch all spots of the world. When you want to know things, sooner or later, you stumble on something special, and that special thing leads you to a full and happy life. Come sit on this side of me, Mrs. Flossie Brooks, and hold my hand while I tell this curious child who I am. You too, child." He motioned to Ola.

Ola leaned in the corner, looking especially green and tired. Izella herself should be looking like that. She was the one who'd been strangled, after all. Ola sat across from them at the table. Izella noticed tiny beads of sweat creeping down the back of her neck and wondered. Her sister looked like the walking dead.

"My daddy's daddy was the first Mr. Melvin Lesley Brooks in the world," he started. "I can't remember much about him. I tell you one thing, though. He did not play." He laughed and leaned back into his memory. "He was a preacher on Sundays and a farmer every other day. His sweet corn grew taller than a five-year-old boy. And his sermons spread so far and wide that, after a while, he didn't have sitting room in his little church.

"He preached about wisdom a whole lot. No matter who you are or where you come from, you want to know how to get more wisdom, and he held the keys in his hands. Wisdom is a muscle in the body, he used to say. Work it?

And it grows like a pecan tree branch toward the Alabama sun. Neglect it? It'll die like a daffodil in the Arizona desert.

"Another thing about Melvin Senior!" He laughed again. "He was a tall glass of too-sweet sweet tea! Ladies used to come from far and wide to catch a look at him. When I was a boy, some of them pretty ladies would ask me about my grandmama. Bold, huh?" He chuckled again and shook his head.

"She didn't go to church with y'all?" Izella asked.

Mr. Melvin sighed and frowned for the first time since she'd known him. "Grandmama's sugars were always out of sorts. Sweet woman. The sweetest I ever met to this day. God dealt her health a bad hand." He forced his chin up and went on. "Let me tell you about my daddy!

"Daddy took after his mama. His kindness, phew . . . never knew a man so kind and patient with young'uns. I dare any man that claims to be as good as my daddy was good. But my mama, Lord, smarter than a whip. Reminds me a little of you, child," he said to Izella. "She was curious, too. Always wanting to know about everything. She was smart before it was accepted for a woman like her to be that."

Just then, Ola's heavy head slumped onto the kitchen table, and she slid out of her chair and onto the floor.

"Ola?" Izella said, wanting to believe she was just tired

from the ride. When she saw a bubbly white foam in the corner of her mouth, she leaped from her seat. "Ola!"

Izella held her sister's head in her lap, and Evangelist squatted down next to them. Izella heard Mr. Melvin calling 911 somewhere off in the distance. The stench of jowl bacon was growing and growing. It must've been in the oven, crackling up and browning for later. It smelled wild. Like the boar had been shot when he was tense. Skilled hunters snuck up from the rear so as not to scare the poor animal before it was shot. Those boars weren't stupid. They knew what the barrel of a shotgun meant. Certain death and stripping down into pieces of ham and tails and jowl. If the hunted caught sight of the hunter, their very last defense was to make themselves tough on the plate. Nature's last-ditch effort at a middle finger.

Ola's whites were showing, and her lashes were fluttering. Little spit bubbles formed and burst at the bow of her lips. The bubbles were tinted purple like Mrs. Mac's elixir.

"Open your eyes, baby," Evangelist said in the saddest voice Izella had ever heard come from anyone. "Let mama see those pretty eyes."

Ola forced her eyes open and looked at Evangelist. "I love you, Mama," she said in a mutter. "Please don't hate me."

Evangelist kissed the back of her hand and said, "Never that."

"Ambulance will be here any minute now," said Mr. Melvin from somewhere in the kitchen. "Hold on there, child."

Ola locked eyes with Izella. "I love you most, Babygal," she said. "Oh, sorry. I'm not supposed to—" She coughed out purple. "I drank it all up. I did it."

Evangelist looked from Ola to Izella, and her sadness turned to anger. "Drank what up, Izella? What is happening to my girl?"

The small kitchen lit up with bright red and blue turning lights. "Where is the patient?" asked a stern male. "Take me to her!"

The whole house smelled like tense bacon and bedlam.

"What is going on?" yelled Evangelist.

A slow sizzle in the background began to grow. That bacon was popping into the bottom of the oven.

"What did you drink?" Evangelist asked Ola, but her eyes had already gone back to white.

Dangerous for that grease and fat to pop all over an open flame in the oven, Izella thought.

"Ma'am," asked the medic frantically. "Did you say this young lady drank something? What did she drink exactly?"

"I'm trying to find out! Can't you see that!"

Pop, pop, pop!

“I’ve got a faint pulse,” said a different medic. “One, two, three, lift!”

They whisked Ola away so fast. Everyone followed alongside except Izella. She stayed on her knees in the kitchen and closed her eyes. Behind her eyelids, she saw herself and Ola on their knees in their own clean kitchen. Peeking at each other while Evangelist prayed too long. Ola really did have beautiful eyes—big as an owl’s with dark, naturally lined lashes made for fluttering. The red and blue lights shrunk and shrunk, and the chaos was over. Izella’s whole world had just blown to bits, and she was left on the floor. She wanted to cry, but she didn’t. It wasn’t her way.

Pop, pop, pop!

She jumped to her feet and went to turn off the stove. Just as she’d guessed it, jowl bacon was burning to a crisp and popping up smoke. With her bare hands, she lifted the pan from the oven. Her palms and fingers hissed and blistered, but she welcomed the pain of it. She deserved it, after all.

MISSIPPI

34 Weeks

The moon had settled overtop the swing set where the Midnight Boys sat laughing and kicking rocks at each other. Her best friend, Sue, had given them that name. It was perfect, and Missippi was grateful to be able to call them something other than the boys on the swings. It made them more real. Before they were just stray kids without mamas and papas to make them go to sleep at a reasonable time. Now they were the Midnight Boys, guardians of the playground. Defenders of the monkey bars and jungle gym.

Everyone else in the apartment was sleeping, and she kept peeking over at Sue, wishing she'd wake up and talk to her. Missippi never thought for a second she'd have a white best friend who loved a man called Johnny Cash and flowers and Joan Baez. Carried around a guitar and hated the war more than Missippi had ever seen anybody hate anything in her whole life. Papa had always told her not to be a follower, but the more Sue told her about that war, the more Missippi was beginning to hate it, too.

Sue had told her about the little Vietnamese kids, even younger than her, being hurt and killed by the president. Before Sue, Missippi hadn't spent too long thinking about the president. She'd seen him on television a few times, looking all stiff and mean. To Missippi, he looked like a blockhead who never wanted to smile, and when he did, his lips seemed to be pulled up by rubber bands. Back in Valdosta, Missippi knew of a bunch of boys who'd come back from the war all twisted in the mind, but she had other things to worry about. Still, it seemed like Sue's whole life was Nixon and Vietnam kids and marching around with that guitar. Her life was an adventure, and all Missippi ever wanted to do was shut her mouth and listen to it.

In the quiet, Missippi heard her babies loud and clear. They fought a lot on the inside. Mostly for space. Whenever they started fighting, Missippi gave them a poke, and they'd stop. That made her feel like a mama telling her young'uns what was what. Her stomach stretched out so much that she couldn't see her feet or knees or the ground a few feet in front of her. If she didn't know better, she'd think she was walking on her belly.

Every morning, the rest of them were awed at how big she'd gotten overnight. She was by far the biggest. Mary's and Lillian's bellies looked like soccer balls, while Sue's could still hide under a big nightshirt. Missippi's, on the other hand, was two basketballs big, maybe two and a half now. Three!

Lying in was easy, though. Ms. Pearline took her pulse so many times a day and listened to the heartbeats all the time. She'd always end with asking how she felt. Missippi felt just fine, but nobody believed her. She'd tell them the truth, no pain or itching or anything, and they all gave her the same look. Like she *must* be hurting and pretending not to be.

Ms. Pearline called her high risk, which Missippi took to mean two babies were a danger. One time, while she was taking heartbeats, Ms. Pearline told her about problems like thin blood, heart issues in the mama, and premature delivery.

That last one had shaken Missippi, since that pretty little wig-snatching, hollering monster of a baby back home named Daisy was a premature girl. She wondered if all premature babies were snake mean like Daisy. Then she prayed in her mind that her babies came right on time. Poor, poor Mrs. Dixie, she thought. Must be so hard to raise up a child like that.

Ms. Pearline kept on asking, twenty times a day, how she was feeling. The only thing Missippi would tell her was about the pee. She peed every second of every minute. One night, she thought about taking a pillow and a cover into the bathroom and going to sleep right there with her bare butt open on the toilet to catch all the pee. The rotten gas had let up, and thank goodness for that. She was beginning to feel bad for Sue, taking the blame all the time.

The Midnight Boys began slapping five and knuckles, which meant they were about to go on home. That was usually Missippi's cue to curl up next to Sue in the bed, but she knew she wouldn't sleep at all that night. Papa was coming up for a visit. He had a drop next door in Indianapolis, and he wanted to see her. He was such a good papa.

He'd want to know who did it to her. He was a dog with a bone, she thought every time he asked. But she would never tell him. Poor Papa might get himself hurt or worse. The only person safe enough to tell was Sue.

Missippi smiled at her best friend, sleeping and snoring a little. Her short hair was starting to grow out, and Lillian had tried to braid it down in the front, but it was too soft and straight to keep. Only one row down the middle kept from slipping, and Sue was so proud of her funny-looking braid that she left it. Missippi laughed and thanked God for a best friend like Sue. Then she rolled her eyes at her familiar urge to pee.

Sometimes she argued with herself about getting up and going to the bathroom. A night of sleep was worth a diamond, rare and beautiful, but her pee barely let her get an hour straight. Two pee voices spoke to her inside her head. One told her she needed to get up and pee, or she'd be embarrassed in front of her friends. But the other voice told her to sleep and pee on herself. She always listened to the first one.

On her way to the bathroom, she noticed wet running down her leg. She sat down, expecting pee, but instead, she found blood. Not much blood, just enough to soak through her panties and reach the middle of her thigh. That had been happening every few days lately, but she never told the others. She didn't know why exactly, except maybe she didn't want to worry them. They were already so worried as it was.

She wiped the blood up, following the trail up her leg,

and stuffed tissue between her legs. The crotch of her panties was nearly black with dark blood. Good sign, she thought. Ms. Pearline said mamas in trouble had thin blood; this was not that at all. Missippi ran the water until it was icy cold and soaked the panties in the sink.

Then she noticed five fully formed toes kicking through the skin of her belly. She smiled and poked her baby's toe. It was strange to see somebody else's foot when she couldn't see her own feet. He was a kicking little something. The other one was a girl, calm and meek. But the boy, have mercy, probably kicked that blood right out of her body.

"Stop it, young'un," she told him. "You messing up all my panties."

He kicked her in response.

"Ouch!" She couldn't help screaming out. She quickly covered her mouth.

"All right in there?" Ms. Pearline hollered. "Any problems?"

"No, Ms. Pearline," Missippi replied. "I'm coming on out."

"I'll check your vitals when you do. Meet me in the kitchen."

She had a gift, Ms. Pearline did. Missippi and Sue had talked about her a lot. She was a saint of a woman—smart, loving, creative, talented. Together, they imagined a different life for Ms. Pearline where she could use all of the gifts God gave her. Well, mostly Sue imagined it while Missippi listened to her. Missippi couldn't see much outside of Valdosta, but Sue had a whole world of knowing to speak on.

Sue said, where she came from, Ms. Pearline could be a traveling nurse. Catching trains from the mountains of Washington to the big city of New York. Healing folks and delivering babies of all kinds. Sue also said Ms. Pearline could marry a rich man if she wanted to, since she was so beautiful. Missippi had told Sue about seeing Ms. Pearline stripped down in her slip once. How she couldn't hardly hold the timer from watching the glow of her skin and hair and face. In the end, Sue said Ms. Pearline would be single. No way she'd sit down to marry a rich man. She could just sleep with men on her travels and change the world for the better. Men were of no use to women like Ms. Pearline. Most men were nothing compared to a strong woman.

That really hit Missippi deep. Men not being important to important girls. It made her think of Unc, and she hated thinking of him. He smelled like hurt and looked like worry. But since he'd been coming to see her, she thought of him that way. Like a sorry excuse for a man.

Missippi didn't know it was okay to think of her elders that way, but Sue did so openly and without being sorry for it.

"You coming?" Ms. Pearline knocked on the bathroom door again.

Missippi flushed, stuffed her wet panties into the breakfront, and hurried out.

•••

The next morning, Missippi popped up from bed, waking everyone. "My papa's coming today, y'all!"

"We know," said Lillian. "You told us twenty thousand times already."

"Let her alone," Sue interjected, and then turned her attention to Missippi. "I'm excited for you, best friend Sippi."

"Thanks, best friend Sue."

"Let me check your pressure," Ms. Pearline called to Missippi. "You were high last night. If your pressure is up, you can't go anywhere today. Just rest."

Missippi felt her eyes grow into saucers and began to breathe deep and slow. She closed her eyes and thought of low blood pressure.

Low blood pressure, low blood pressure, low blood pressure.

Inside her head, she told her babies to say it with her.

Low blood pressure, low blood pressure, low blood pressure.

She laughed at their little voices chanting along with her on the inside. She hadn't told another soul she could hear them, not even best friend Sue. They might well think she'd lost it. She also hadn't told anyone that she was having one boy and one girl. That seemed like a sacred thing to tell. Like telling a birthday wish after blowing out all the candles.

Missippi got up and walked slowly to Ms. Pearline's blood pressure cuff. Everybody was watching them, waiting for the results like a game of baseball. Missippi saw best friend Sue crossing her fingers, and she was thankful to her for that.

"Relax." Ms. Pearline smiled and placed the cuff around her upper arm. "And don't move."

"I think she knows the drill by now," said Lillian. "Ouch!"

"Shut up, now," Mary said after elbowing her in the side. "Good luck, Missippi."

The cuff squeezed lightly and then kept on squeezing until it kind of hurt. Missippi liked the feel of it. After a time, it released with a huff of wind.

"All right," said Ms. Pearline. "One forty-three over one oh nine."

"Woooooo!" they all yelled out.

"Still a little high, but you can go. Just take it easy," Ms. Pearline added. "No excitement."

"When will Papa be here?"

"Any minute now, I'd say."

Missippi hollered at the sound of a knock on the door, and Ms. Pearline hushed her cautiously.

"Who's there?" she asked.

"Who you think, Pearl?"

Ms. Pearline rushed them into her bedroom and told them to lock themselves inside. Missippi knew not to like this man. He was what Sue would call a loser.

"Hey there, Mr. Reese," Ms. Pearline said. "I left your money in the box. You get it?"

Missippi hated to hear Ms. Pearline speak like that. She didn't even sound like herself. She sounded like a lady trying to make a bad man feel like a better man.

"I got your money," he said, obviously unsatisfied. "I'm just coming by to make sure everything working up here."

"Everything's working fine, Mr. Reese. Thank you."

"That toilet flushes so much it's bound to break soon."

Ms. Pearline giggled in a way she did only when he stopped by. "Women go more than men—you know that, silly goose."

"It's them girls in here," he said with a slur. "Shitting and pissing up the whole building. And who has to fix the plumbing when they mess it up? You're looking at him. You ain't paying me near enough."

"I don't have any more, Mr. Reese."

"How many girls you got back there?" he spat. "Let me see them."

"Oh, Mr. Reese," Ms. Pearline said with a nervous chuckle. "Am I not enough for you?"

"I mean it, Pearl. Now."

"Hi there, ma'am," said another male voice.

"Papa," Missippi whispered to the girls. "He's saving us."

Mary, Lillian, and Sue all held their fingers to their mouths to hush her up. Missippi bounced on her heels. Papa was a good papa, but she didn't know he was a superhero, too. Come to save the day.

"I'll be back later on, Pearl," said Mr. Reese before stomping off.

"Sorry 'bout that," said Papa. "I didn't mean to . . ."

"No." Ms. Pearline's voice returned to normal. "Please don't apologize. You actually . . . never mind. Missippi will be along. Do you want some tea?"

"Sure, I'll take tea."

Missippi got tickled at Papa accepting Ms. Pearline's

unsweet tea. He liked his tea sweet as cane, and Ms. Pearline's was bitter and nasty. She wanted to wait and jump out soon as he took his first sip. To see his twisted-up face when he tasted that mess. So she and the others stayed put in the bedroom for a few more minutes.

"Who was that man?" he asked Ms. Pearline. "Didn't give off nothing nice."

"Oh," said Ms. Pearline, trying to sound normal and failing. "That's just the handyman, Tim Reese. He comes by from time to time to check on things."

"Pardon, ma'am," Papa started. "But I know his kind from back in Georgia. Hound full of drunk courage and rabid. I'll be glad to give him a quick talking-to if you like."

Papa sounded drawn out and country. Missippi hadn't noticed it before. Probably since she was surrounded by drawn-out and country folks back home. But now that she lived in the middle of northerners, she heard every bit of Valdosta in his voice.

"That means a lot really, but he'll just come back as soon as you head out. I'm taking care of him."

"My only child is here with you, Ms. Pearline," Papa said sternly. "And my grandbaby, too. I wouldn't be doing it for you."

"Missippi is perfectly safe here, sir. I assure you," Ms.

Pearline said, matching his stern tone. "I take the life and health of these young ladies seriously. I would gladly lay down my own for them without as much as a blink. Also, sir," she said, significantly softening her tone, "I thought Missippi would have told you. You have more than one grandchild coming. She's having twins."

A sweet silence came over the small apartment. Sue shook Missippi's shoulder and Mary shimmied. Lillian pressed her ear closer to the door for Papa's reaction.

Papa broke through by saying, "Two babies?"

"Two babies," Ms. Pearline repeated after him. "That's right. She's high risk, so I've been paying close attention to her breathing and movement. While I'm thinking of it, I have an important question to ask you. Does Missippi ever embellish the truth about her own health? For instance, ever say she's fine when she's obviously not?"

Missippi thought about bursting through the door to interrupt them, but she was curious what Papa's answer would be. She was guilty, without a doubt. But did Papa know it? she wondered. The fact that Ms. Pearline did came as a shock. With Missippi not having a mama, she didn't understand the gifts of women. Were they all that shrewd about other people's thoughts? Those kinds of moments came up from time to time.

"Missippi has never told me a story," Papa said. "If she

don't want me to know, she won't tell it, but she won't tell a bold-faced lie."

"Not even a little white one to protect you?"

There was a long gap of quiet in the apartment. Missippi thought of little lies she'd thought no one had noticed. Like the one about understanding the Bible from the front to back cover. And the one about her paper dolls being company enough while Papa was out of town. And not to mention the one about her liking the pickled eggs he brought her home from his travels. She'd eat them in his face and smile before throwing them right back up in the toilet. Lies were okay as long as they were for good. Little white lies, as Ms. Pearline had called them.

"Maybe," said Papa. "I don't know. What is this you gave me here? I think your tea has gone bad."

Missippi took that as her cue to enter. "Papa!" She leaped toward him like she always had, but it hurt a little in the low belly.

"My God," Papa said, holding her at an arm's length.

He hadn't been by since he'd dropped her off all those weeks ago. She'd grown quite a bit. Missippi had never seen her papa cry. But there he was, crying like a little baby. His whole face went upside down like he'd been dipped in gloom. He threw his head back and forth in a tantrum and wailed like he'd been holding it in. Missippi wanted to take him away from there. Nobody should see him cry like that, but if anybody was going to see, she was glad it was them. They were family, too, after all.

"Who did this to you, baby?" He was all snot and drool and tears.

"Come on, girls," said Sue. "Let's give them some privacy."

Then Missippi began to cry. "Wait," she said blubbering. "Papa, this is best friend Sue. And other best friends, Mary and Lillian. And you know Ms. Pearline already. They been God's gifts to my life. Oh! And the Midnight Boys coming along before too long!" She ran over to the window. "They must be sleep now, though."

He looked up, and again he asked, "Who did this to you?"

"Papa, you a broken record now!" Missippi said to him. "Here! Listen to best friend Sue play this Johnny Cash–man song. You know him, Papa?"

"I know him," Papa hiccuped. "He's playing in my rig right now."

"How did you not tell me about Johnny Cash?" Missippi folded her arms. "His songs are stories. Fun ones! That man's been everywhere! Just like you, Papa."

Papa wiped his face and smiled. "Sorry, ladies," he said. "I just ain't expect . . ."

"She's carrying twins," Ms. Pearline interjected softly. "And she's carrying them right out front. Soon as she has them, her little body will go right back to where it was before. Of this I have no doubt."

"See, Papa?" She wiggled him into a snotty hug. "Ms. Pearline is smart as a whip, and if she says I'll go right back to where I was before, it's right."

"Well, then, Ms. Pearline," he started. "Is it safe to take my girl out to get some ice cream?"

"Oh, please, please, please," Missippi said. "I only been out a few times and never past the playground. Can I?"

Ms. Pearline nodded to Missippi and then locked eyes with Papa. "If you notice any shortness of breath or swelling in the ankles, bring her right back here. Also . . ." Ms. Pearline grabbed two of his snotty fingers and placed them onto Missippi's neck. "Count the beats for me. Aloud."

"One, two, three, four, five . . ."

"Okay, stop," she said. "Start again."

"One, two, three, four, five . . ."

"Okay, stop," she repeated. "Start again."

"One, two, three, four, five . . ."

"Okay," she said finally. "See how slowly you're counting? If you feel yourself counting faster than that, bring her right back. I want you to do that at least every thirty minutes. Got it?"

Papa nodded and looked over at his daughter with worry all over him. "I won't forget."

• • •

Papa helped Missippi onto the train. Everyone gawked as she waddled down the aisle. She smiled at them just like she would do at home in Valdosta, but most of them didn't smile back. Instead, they pretended not to see her at all. So rude, she thought. Mary had told her people in the city weren't too kind. But Missippi knew that sometimes mean people just needed a little love. A smile from a stranger or a two-step biscuit if they're really having a rough go of things.

"Sit down here, Sippi," Papa said. "Easy there, slowly."

Papa handled her like a porcelain doll.

"I'm okay, Papa. Don't make a fuss."

Papa cleared his throat the way he did when he was remembering something important. "Ms. Pearline told me you might do that from time to time. Is she right about that?"

Missippi knew that he meant the little white lies. She didn't want to lie to his face about whether or not she ever lied to his face. God's honest truth was yes. Ms. Pearline had her dead to rights. But how does a girl tell her papa she's a little white liar?

"Papa." Missippi reached for his hand. "You're a good papa. And I don't never want you to worry about nothing."

"So you do tell me stories sometimes?" he asked sadly. "I won't be mad if you do, Sippi."

"Only when it might hurt you to tell it."

Papa leaned back, slumping into the curve of the seat. The intercom announced the next stop. Hegewisch Station. Such a strange name. Missippi wondered how to spell it.

"I need you to tell me the whole truth, Sippi. Are you hurting and not telling Ms. Pearline?"

Missippi searched herself for pain and quickly found it in her low belly. It had been coming and going since night, but it was easy to ignore since it didn't last long. She didn't want to lie, so she waited for the pain to pass again before she answered. "No, Papa," she said without lying. "I feel fine right now."

He placed two fingers on the side of her neck. "One, two, three, four, five. One, two, three, four, five. One, two, three, four, five. Okay, let's get ready to get off."

Missippi bounced with joy. "Where you taking me, Papa?"

He forced his face right side up. "I'm taking my baby to Margie's ice cream shop. Best in the wide world."

The world grew by a hundred when Missippi stepped off the train. She counted six lanes of traffic zooming past her and so many different types of people everywhere. She tried to count them, but there were too many of them. A man with a Panama hat bumped Papa's shoulder and excused himself. A lady in a short red dress crossed the white lines of the street, and everybody watched her do it. An older lady in a walker sat alone at the bus stop with bags at her feet.

"Papa." Missippi tugged at his jacket. "Should we help that nice old lady along?"

Papa laughed a little. "This is Chicago, Sippi. If that woman made it this long here, she could probably help us more than we can help her."

The feeble-looking woman popped up from the bus bench, grabbed her bags on her forearm, and boarded the bus like it was her second home. Papa was right. Stronger than she looked. When the woman's bus drove on ahead, Missippi noticed a group of strangers pointing at her babies with their mouths open. This time, she didn't smile at them. She knew judgment when she saw it. She gave them a scowl instead.

"Ignore them, Sippi," said Papa before rubbing the top of her head. "What flavor you want?"

Missippi tried to do as her papa said. She would've been

able to, but they weren't pointing at her. They were pointing at her two young'uns. They hadn't bothered nobody. Except maybe each other with all the kicking. Baby girl and baby boy already been pointed at like they don't have the right to get a scoop of ice cream like everybody else. Missippi felt protective of them. She wanted to line up those fools and give them all a hard slap across the cheek.

"Come on, Sippi." Papa encouraged her to cross the street. She did, but she was still angry. "Your first lesson of being a parent: Sometimes you got to walk away from the foolishness."

"You think I'm a parent, Papa?"

He looked away and didn't answer her. "You never told me what flavor you want?"

"What flavor they got?"

"They got everything you can dream of. Go ahead," he replied. "Call one out."

"Chocolate?"

"Sippi, that's easy. Of course they do."

"Butter pecan?"

"Yep."

"Mint chocolate?"

"They got it."

"Pickled flavor?"

"Ahh," Papa said. "I think you got me on that one."

Papa held the door open and guided her under the bright red, striped awning. The place was buzzing with people. Papa spotted a large, mustard-colored booth and claimed it. "Sit down here, Sippi. I'm going to get you a chocolate, butter pecan, mint chocolate sundae. And I'll see what I can do on pickles."

Missippi laughed and began bouncing until it hurt too badly. The pains in her low belly were getting a little stronger and more regular, but they were still tolerable. She'd been holding her instinct to cringe at them. When Papa turned his back to order, she allowed herself to shudder in pain. Breathe, she told herself. Breathe, she told her little girl. Breathe, she told her little boy.

Papa returned with three different scoops in a bowl and a pickle spear sticking through the top. His face dropped when he saw her. She wasn't quick enough to hide her cringe.

"I'm fine, Papa."

Instead of a reply, he placed his two fingers on her neck and counted. "One, two, three, four, five. One, two, three, four, five. One, two, three, four, five. Let's go."

"But what about my ice cream?"

"Let's go," he said firmly. "Now."

•••

They took a bright yellow taxi back to Ms. Pearline's place instead of the bus. Missippi couldn't believe how much money it cost poor Papa. She vowed to pay him back as soon as she could. It was her fault for making all that fuss.

"What's wrong?" Ms. Pearline answered the door without as much as a hello.

"Her heartbeat was real fast," Papa said frantically. "And I think you right about her lying. I caught her looking like she was hurting bad."

"Mississippi." Ms. Pearline said her full name in an angry roar. "How much does it hurt, on a scale of one to ten?"

"Uh . . ." Missippi searched her body again for pain. "Two?"

"Mississippi!" Ms. Pearline yelled outright. "It's important that you tell me the truth here. Has the pain been coming in waves? Hurting at a two and then hurting at a . . . say . . . ten?"

Missippi nodded.

"How long as this been happening?" she asked as she rushed to prepare the bed, laying down plastic squares and blankets, just like she had done for Ruby weeks ago. "How long?" she screamed, and Missippi jumped at the outburst.

"Since last night."

Ms. Pearline shot her a look of horror and fury that made her cower.

"Sippi," said Sue. "Oh, no."

"Have you bled?" Ms. Pearline was frenzied and nervous now.

"I . . ." Missippi began. "A little."

"Have you had water?"

Missippi nodded. It had happened on the toilet last night.

"Come here, girl. Lay down overtop of this plastic so I can check your labor," Ms. Pearline said, shaking. "Have you lost your membrane?"

"What's that mean?" Missippi asked as Papa, best friend Sue, Lillian, and Mary laid her down on the bed.

"It's a thick plug. Like slow slime coming out."

"I didn't see that."

"Are you lying again?" Ms. Pearline demanded. "Did you see it or not?"

"No, ma'am."

Ms. Pearline opened Missippi's knees and set what felt like her whole hand inside her. Missippi couldn't stop herself from yelling out.

"Lillian, Mary," Ms. Pearline instructed. "Get the stick from the kitchen and place it in her teeth. Sue, get the chicken timer from the kitchen counter, next to the pepper grinder. This child is in active labor."

"What should I do, ma'am?" Papa asked in the most terrified voice Missippi'd ever heard out of him.

Ms. Pearline replied without looking up. "That's for you and your daughter to decide. You can wait back in my bedroom or you can hold her hand while she brings these babies into the world. Decide now, though. This is happening soon."

Papa looked into his daughter's eyes. "Sippi," he said. "My sweet baby girl."

"Papa." Sippi could barely get his name out through the thick pain.

"I'd like to stay here with you."

Missippi felt a tear fall from the corner of her eye. "You're such a good papa."

SUE

23 Weeks

The very first time she heard her dear sweet Missippi refer to her as "best friend Sue," she thought it was a one-time thing, but hoped it wasn't. Stankybooty was getting old after all.

Best friend Sippi hung on her every word. Listening intently to her stories about marches and protests and Richard-fucking-Nixon. Sue left out the *fucking*, though. Best friend Sippi was too sugary sweet for such sour language, and Sue didn't want to be responsible for spoiling her.

Sue could go on and on with Sippi. Sometimes the others rolled their eyes at them, loving each other so much. But Sue didn't care. They were soul mates, like in the best books she'd ever read—Bennet and Darcy, Eowyn and Faramir, Gatsby and Buchanan. Two kindred spirits finding each other in the crowded world. Better than gold, she was. The only thing Sue couldn't talk about to Sippi was her mother, Margaret.

Sue never really talked about her mother to anyone, actually, but with Sippi, it felt like an especially unkind thing to do. Even the smallest mention of a mother in the apartment perked her ears. She was a girl longing for a mother figure, that much was beyond obvious to Sue. And if she dared complain or brag about her own, that might hurt her. Though the avoidance of it was becoming difficult, since Sue's mother sent letters. When the first one had come, Ms. Pearline announced it to everyone at lunchtime.

"Sue," she said before handing her the unopened envelope. "Your mother sent a beautiful letter."

Sue noticed Sippi watching the letter as if it held the answers to years of questions. Then her eyes lost their glow. She wanted beautiful letters for herself. Sue tucked it under herself and pinched Sippi's cheek to perk her up, but it was no use. She moped for hours afterward.

That night, Sue had a talk with Ms. Pearline. Asking her to hide the letters on top of the cupboard so Sippi couldn't see them. Ms. Pearline told her knowingly, "Good idea, Sue. Good idea."

•••

One night, after Sippi had fallen asleep, Sue edged a chair to the cupboard and retrieved the letters. She was surprised to see them separated into two stacks.

There she sat, hidden behind the island in the middle of the kitchen floor with unread letters at her feet. She organized them by date and then smelled them. They smelled like her mother, dainty and understated. The first had been sent the week she'd arrived, and there was a crisp hundred-dollar bill in it. Sue tucked the money between her growing breasts and read the salutation: *Dear Susan, I've always wanted to tell you this.* Then she gave herself permission to open only two more. It was all she could take in one night.

The salutations read like beautiful confessions written in careful cursive:

Dear Susan,

I've always wanted to tell you this…

Dear Susan,

I could never find the appropriate words...

Dear Susan,

I fear I may owe you an apology...

For some reason, Sue was nervous to begin reading them in their entirety. She did so anyway:

Dear Susan,

I've always wanted to tell you this. First of all, darling, I love you so very much. Secondly, I am not good at sharing my thoughts aloud with anyone, and I never have been.

When I was in school, many people thought me mute. As a very young child, I decided to take a sabbatical from speaking. To your grandparents' chagrin, I didn't speak a word for an entire year of my life. I would have gladly gone on longer if they hadn't threatened institutionalization.

On the Vineyard, children are expected to be perfect and check all of the boxes. Beauty, class, intellect, culture, and the ability to speak. Since I did not possess the last of them, they assumed me less than smart and lacking culture. Beauty, the least important of virtues in my opinion, has always been out of my control. Mother's genes gave me that without effort. But I longed for knowledge and culture above all other things. In my lifelong search for them, what I found surprised me—passion. But alas, I never found my ability to speak those passions aloud.

You, darling, have what I always wanted—the skill to debate your own ideas. This is why I am so lenient with your curfews and social life. I am in no way oblivious to the things you've been up to. I know about the young men you've marched with and slept with. I know that you're a paying member of numerous Democratic organizations. And most of all, I know how much you hate this war. And maybe even hate your own father for this war.

Still, call me naive, I was honestly shocked when you told me about your condition. I believe parents should trust their children with their own sexual lives, and I expected that you would utilize protection.

However, I have had time to consider your side of things. And, more importantly, reflect on my own youth. I, too, made unwise decisions at your age. Those I may reveal in subsequent letters, but as of now, I am not ready.

This first letter will be to express the love that I feel for you, despite your choices. Darling, there is nothing you can do to avoid my love. It may move mountains.

Your mother,

Margaret Claire Laura Hurley-Day

P.S. I sincerely hope you love Ms. Pearline as much as I do. I've been following her cause for years, and she is, bar none, better and more capable than anyone in and around the state of Illinois. If, by chance, you experience anything out of sorts, find a phone and call. Night or day, darling.

Sue saw a smear at the end, likely caused by her mother's tears. Her heart ached for her mother, and she felt a rumble of pain inside her. While her morning sickness had passed weeks ago, she still experienced phantom flips and turns in her abdomen. This, however, was that unfamiliar feeling of regret.

Sue usually had a policy of never regretting anything, since every decision, even the bad ones, led to the full human experience. But she should have used a condom, like her mother had mentioned.

Sue knew the night she'd gotten pregnant. It was after a small rally Michael had arranged at their school. Her ex-boyfriend Malcolm Engel was staring at her longingly from across the practice field, holding too many books. He was a scholarship kid, attending their school because he was brilliant, not because he was rich. He was penniless, actually. But still, Sue loved Malcolm, and in retrospect, she had no idea why she'd dumped him the week before. She'd taken his virginity while he still wore his large glasses. With Malcolm, she had used a condom. With Michael a week later, she hadn't.

She turned it over and over in her mind. Why had she done this to herself? Handcuffed herself to the asshole, while letting go of the good one a week before. Regret brought back the sickness in her gut. She pulled out the next letter to focus on something else.

Dear Susan,

I could never find the appropriate words until this moment. This may be a faux pas for a mother to tell this to her daughter about her father, but I do not agree with his politics. I've tried very hard to hide it from you. Forcing myself to smile when I want to act out, which happens quite often actually. I believe that history will frown upon him and his president.

Please know that I am not revealing this for any reason other than to help you understand me. I have not been open enough with you over the years, and I'm ready to alter that.

Your mother,

Margaret Claire Laura Hurley-Day

Sue eagerly opened the next one.

Dear Susan,

I fear I may owe you an apology. I wrote the last letter after drinking too much wine.

My apologies,

Margaret Claire Laura Hurley-Day

P.S. Though I must add, it was the truth. ☺

Sue had to cover her mouth so she didn't laugh out loud. Over the years, she'd guessed her mother secretly felt this way, but never thought she'd ever reveal it to her. After the initial shot of amusement, Sue began reflecting on her parents' relationship. No hugging or kissing on the mouth that she could remember. They'd always greeted each other by air-kisses on the cheek and pleasant nods of mutual acknowledgment. Even if he'd been gone for weeks, that was their greeting—sterile and loveless.

Sue knew that if she married a boy like Michael, she'd be doomed to live a life like that. With Malcolm, they could grow together. Build something strong with a firm foundation. But with Michael, the father of this baby, the future had been set through generational wealth and privilege. A future of beige, colorless Kenilworth. A future with a man just like the one she hated the most—her horrible father. Maybe her father couldn't stand her mother, either. He was probably having an affair back in DC.

Sue could vaguely remember a time when she liked her father. He'd always been obsessively competitive about everything. Blindly competitive. So much so, in fact, while playing board games, he couldn't see the hatred emitting from the person across from him. He cared only for the win. Never for the person he was playing with, even his seven-year-old daughter.

Sue once played a four-hour game of Monopoly with him. Not only did he kick her butt, he also rubbed it in by spending the final hour explaining why she'd lost. To seven-year-old Sue, it'd been equally infuriating and endearing. She viewed him as a misguided teacher. And loved him in spite of his flaws.

The moment she began to hate him was the same moment she realized there was no point to the war he supported. The two things converged on her like a supernova. Her beloved father was playing a competitive game of Monopoly with people's lives. Desperate to win, win, win, and then tell broken children's parents why he had the right to break them. But there he was. Safe and sound on a cot in his office or in his Washington apartment. Or with some secret family in the suburbs of DC. The pits.

She hurried to open another letter to take her mind off him.

Dear Susan,

One summer in Chappaquiddick, I slept with a young man named Harry. He lived in Boston and had no money to speak of. He finagled his way into the Vineyard crowd with personality and usefulness. He'd been accepted into Harvard Law and likely knew more than any of the professors there. Harry was brilliant. Not handsome, not rich, but brilliant. His mind set him apart.

I loved him.

My sisters did not. They were relentless with their disdain. They told me that if I married him, I'd live in a small condominium in South Boston and raise ten Catholic children in rags. At first when they told me this, I fantasized about it. Besides, I never liked sanitary rooms in large houses. As a very young child, all those rooms scared me. But at some point, their words crept into my consciousness.

I left him for your father. On our wedding day, my sisters were grinning bridesmaids, and we moved into an enormous home with no soul. He sat cross-legged at the knee and sipped tea.

I tell you this, darling, because I see my life repeating in you. Your young

Malcolm reminds me of my young Harry. I liked Malcolm very much. I never told you. I am so very sorry I didn't tell you. I should have formed my lips to say the words as I write them now.

I cannot tell you what the future holds for you, darling. I wish I had a crystal ball. But I needed to let you know about this.

I hope all is well with you. Again, please do not hesitate to call if you would like to talk. Anytime day or night.

Your mother,

Margaret Claire Laura Hurley-Day

P.S. Harry teaches law at Harvard today. Isn't that something?

Sue's initial instinct was anger. Such valuable information shared six months too late. One more letter, she thought.

Dear Susan,

I spoke with Michael's parents today. The three of them came by to sit for tea this afternoon. I would like to begin by saying, with full candor, that I do not like them in the least. They are snobs who wear fur wraps in the summer.

Having said that, they came with a proposition. They began by laying out their plans for their son, if you care. He will take over his grandfather's business, which comes with what they referred to as a fair amount of international notoriety. Therefore, they would like you to consider adoption. His father insisted they pay for the best adoption attorney in the country. And his mother insisted they pay for the best medical care in the country. All in all, they would like to whisk you away to an oceanfront facility to give birth and give the baby to, as they called it, the best family in the country.

Apparently, they have access to the best of the best of everything available in the country. However, I told them, with as much kindness as I could muster, to fuck off. Then they pulled an ace, darling. Well, young Michael did. He's threatened to call your father.

Again, I must reiterate that I do not like this family in the least.

I wanted very much to keep this from you, darling. But I fear my secrecy has contributed to our current predicament. Please know that I am working every moment of every day to figure this out, and I will keep you abreast of everything as it happens.

Your mother,
Margaret Claire Laura Hurley-Day

As Sue went to open the next letter, she heard Sippi whisper for her. "Sue?"

She was turning in her sleep again. Sippi had never slept a full night without the nightmares, and lately, she'd been calling out to Sue like a child would her mother. Sue jumped to take a seat at her side if she fully woke up.

She went for her guitar to play something small and soothing. Without thinking, her fingers picked where they wanted until a song formed—

I look at you all, see the love there that's sleeping

While my guitar gently weeps

The Beatles had never been her favorite. Not even in her top ten actually, but that song was Sue's perfect foe. A trick song that sounds like a lullaby, but it made her want to break her favorite guitar. Even the pieces in the middle were faultlessly placed in the offbeat. "While My Guitar

Gently Weeps" could test the best artists in its complicated simplicity. By the fourth line, she forgot the lyrics and started to cry.

"What's wrong, best friend Sue?" Only Missippi's large eyes peeked from under the covers. Her stomach seemed to grow larger every time Sue looked at her.

Sue's body filled with every possible emotion. Hatred for Missippi's uncle for raping an innocent, and her father for going away on such long trips, and her mother for dying, and Michael for being the entitled, poser father of the baby inside Sue's own body. Sadness for her mother's lost words, and best friend Sippi, and all those kids in Vietnam. Regret for Malcolm. But mostly, in that moment, she felt pity for the unborn children in that room. Where would they all end up?

She'd never given herself permission to think of that before. But Michael's entitled family was determining where hers was going while sipping tea. So many babies with no destination. How many babies must there be like this in the world? Abortion was very much illegal. Girls had to have their babies and put them somewhere. But where?

Four girls in an apartment. Waiting to bring life into the world. Waiting like clueless cattle chewing blades of grass as they looped around the conveyor belt. Knowing better than to question what comes next. She looked at the three of them, all awake now. All with concerned eyes.

Mary. In love with a boy back home. At least she had hope for something beautiful. A little family with someone who might just step up.

Lillian. Strong-willed and pretending to be more sure of herself than she actually was.

Best friend Sippi. Innocent. Only innocent.

And herself.

She looked at them, one after another. "What will happen to us? After?"

They all reached for their respective stomachs like a chorus of floating hands. Even Sue lifted her guitar to rub at hers. It was there, no doubt about it. Small but there. And as if on cue, the thing inside her kicked her hand for the first time. She must've jumped, because three brown hands also lunged for her front as well.

"Whoa, mama." Lillian softly rubbed Sue's flipping belly. "You've got a strong one in there."

•••

Sue woke to the smell of coffee. At first she was excited to breathe it in. But then she remembered that Ms. Pearline only ever brewed decaffeinated.

Everyone else was awake and standing around Ms. Pearline, painting in the corner. From her vantage point, Sue couldn't see the picture. She could only see the expressions on their faces. It must have been magical. Sippi was bouncing on her heels like she did when something truly spectacular was happening. And both Mary's and Lillian's mouths were so cavernous, an entire Oreo could fit. Though Sue made noise, no one noticed she was awake. They were watching the painting.

Ms. Pearline looked like she was in a trance. That was familiar to Sue. She'd seen the same look when she went to see the Carpenters live. A spell came over the stage from the moment they stepped on until they left. That level of artistry was only achieved by the best among us. Sue longed for it. When she walked over to see the painting, she understood.

A colorless canvas. Only tiny gray stripes making up the whole. Four girls with eyes too large to fit on their faces. All full term. All holding on tight to one another. All looking straight ahead. The landscape behind them exploding. Trees stripped of their leaves, wood floating up into ash, clouds of gray smoke billowing at their heels. But they stared ahead, strong and determined to keep moving.

"It's . . . us."

Ms. Pearline did not reply; she instead kept frantically drawing, as if she'd lose the vision if she paused to explain it. Her hands moved back and forth, up and down so quickly. Sue glued her lips together, intuitively knowing that she was witnessing pure brilliance happening feet in front of her.

How could such a woman exist? Sue thought. She could be famous. An Eleanor Roosevelt. An institution of a woman. An inspiration to so many. Sue had attended galas for lesser women. Ms. Pearline could be anything she wanted in the world, and she chose to hide away with pregnant girls in her small apartment. For some reason, Sue became angry at her wasted potential. A painter. A nurse. A midwife. A doula. A teacher. A rare beauty. All hidden.

Ms. Pearline's wrist slowed and finally came to a stop. The picture was done and powerful. Unlike anything else Sue had seen in her life.

When Ms. Pearline spoke, she sounded tired and scared. Nervous, like she got from time to time. "I heard you all last night. I tried not to, but I did."

Sippi placed her small hand overtop Ms. Pearline's. "That's okay. We eavesdrop on you all the time."

Everyone in the room laughed at that except Ms. Pearline. Instead, she moved over to sit on the side of the unmade bed. "I would like to tell you girls what will ultimately happen to your babies, but I have no idea. It's what I'm most afraid of. Some of my girls have gone with adoption. While others have raised their little ones."

"How many girls have you had in here?" Sue asked before sitting next to her.

"Thirty-three before you four," she replied, and pointed to Lillian. "You're thirty-four." Then Mary. "Thirty-five." Then best friend Sippi. "Thirty-six." And finally Sue. "Thirty-seven. All successful pregnancies and births. Most of my girls write afterward. You become my family, you see?"

"The ones who raise they babies," Sippi started. "They're happy they did that?"

"It depends," Ms. Pearline answered honestly. "On resources and family support. I have one girl who decided to keep her baby boy on her daddy's farm, and now he's plowing and harvesting right along with everyone else. Then, there are others who struggle."

Ms. Pearline didn't want to elaborate, that much was obvious to Sue. "What's the best ending you've heard from one of your girls?" Sue asked to take the pressure off.

Ms. Pearline smiled gratefully. "One of my girls graduated recently and went on to community college. I wasn't at all surprised. She was smart as a whip. She and her mother took shifts with the baby, and she's studying to be a nurse. In her last letter, she said she wants to be like me."

"That's nice," said Sippi with a pat on the back. "You're a good one to want to be like."

"I suppose." Ms. Pearline hunched her shoulders. "But I didn't choose the easiest life for myself, did I?"

"Come on, Ms. Pearline." Mary grabbed her by the hand and led her toward the kitchen sink. "Let's get this dark paint off."

Lillian dragged a chair behind them and shoved it under Ms. Pearline while Sippi wet a thick yellow sponge with warm water and Dial soap. Lillian then peeled Ms. Pearline's large sweater off, and Mary crouched down to take off her shoes. Sue stood motionless, watching Ms. Pearline allow them to remove one article of clothing after the other until she was in her slip.

Sippi had been correct. Ms. Pearline looked like a woman who belonged on the front of a magazine. Or reigning as Miss America. She could sit right next to her mother, Margaret, in Chappaquiddick and fit in like a white lace glove.

Ms. Pearline closed her eyes and cried as three pregnant girls carefully sponged the paint from underneath what was left of her bitten fingernails. And Mary, after filling a small tub with warm, soapy water, massaged circles into the bottoms of her feet.

"My mama says there's a soul living under the sole of every walking woman's feet. Needs to be washed and rubbed every now and then to keep her going." Mary looked up at Sue. "Play."

And Sue did.

Her nemesis, "While My Guitar Gently Weeps," flowed from her crying lips like caramel. The four of them waded through the song together in the apartment, showering this wonderful woman with so much less than she deserved. She deserved Carnegie Hall. The Met. She deserved the whole world for what she'd done to improve it. But this would have to do. Sue, Mary, Lillian, and best friend Sippi would have to be enough that day.

• • •

Later that night, after everyone had fallen asleep, Sue went back to her letters. The last one she'd read was about Michael. Fucking poser Michael. Liar Michael. Snob-running-behind-his-grandmama Michael. Sue hoped this one would be about her mother, not him. She'd been itching to know her mother more ever since she'd opened the first letter the night before.

Dear Susan,

I've just realized that I may have left you on a bit of a cliffhanger. In the very first letter, I included a hundred-dollar bill. This must have come as quite a shock, seeing that you cannot get out to purchase anything. In order to adequately explain this, I need to tell you a shocking bit from my childhood.

When I was seventeen, I gave birth to a son. My mother, your grandmother of course, sent me to a beautiful plantation in Adelaide. I received the best possible care there in Australia. Surrounded by roses, we took walking field trips to museums and central markets. The nurses wore bonnets and ironed dresses. It cost a fortune. I know this for certain, because I roomed with two of the wealthiest young women I've met in my life to date. One, daughter of an English aristocrat, and the *other, a cousin within the royal family. We were tucked away, you see? Hidden from the ever-prying eyes of the wealthy.*

We became close. Actually, I loved them more than I've ever loved any man. Almost as much as I love you, darling. They were my soul mates in life. But alas, after we gave birth, our trio disbanded and scattered across the world.

A few years ago, when I found out about Ms. Pearline's mission, I reached out to her in earnest. She reminded me very much of the most beautiful piece of life in Adelaide, because she was a young apprentice there while I was a patient. We've been meeting on the third Tuesday of every month for years. I support her cause because I believe in it. I sent you to her, not to Adelaide, because I believe in Ms. Pearline. I ask you, darling, do not mention this to anyone.

Now, the hundred-dollar bill is for a man called Timothy Reese. She has told me of him. If, by some chance, he catches sight of you, give him the money and get home as soon as you can. Keep it with you, at the ready if he makes a scene. This is especially important, darling.

Now, as for the boy I birthed. To answer the inevitable question, I do not know where he ended up. Back then, a young girl's singular option was blind adoption. I held him to my chest for mere minutes before the nurses whisked him away. Ms. Pearline stayed with me. Held me as I cried a flood. Please do not ask any more about this chapter of my life, darling. It is truly quite painful.

Your mother,

Margaret Claire Laura Hurley-Day

P.S. I named him Harry, after his father. Though, alas, I doubt they kept his name.

Sue went blank. My mother had another child, Sue thought. A boy in Adelaide. Ms. Pearline had been there with her. Loving her. Caring for her. There was so much she did not understand about her mother. She was an enigma.

Something clicked in her mind. The summer they vacationed in Adelaide. The beaches were so beautiful, they looked like they were blanketed with diamonds. And the people were sugary sweet to them, waving and smiling as they passed. Sue remembered being treated like royalty there. She wanted to see the kangaroos, so her mother told the tour guide to take her to a place called Kangaroo Island, where the open woodlands were littered with them. It had been one of Sue's favorite places to visit in the world. But she always wondered why her mother hadn't gone with her to see the kangaroos.

She'd probably gone to the place she'd given birth to her first child. How was her pregnancy? How many hours was she in labor? Did she regret deciding on adoption? Did she wish she'd kept her son? Had she gone looking for him afterward? Had she looked for the other two girls? If they were from such prominent families, they'd likely have been easy enough to track down.

It was as if her mother had been waiting for her to become pregnant and be sent away so she could confess her life to her. The more she wrote, the more Sue realized just how alive her mother was on the inside. Unable to speak with confidence, but utterly alive anyway.

How horrible it must be for her, Sue thought. Not being able to vocalize her words when she needed them. Her letters, though, were brilliant, succinct, and powerful. She should write everything down and hand out letters to everyone she knows, Sue thought. Or, better yet, write a book as an outlet. Tell her truths and change all the names.

Still, there were so many questions Sue wanted to ask. Not only of her mother but of Ms. Pearline, too. She folded her arms, knowing how hard it had been for her mother to write that letter. Sue carefully tucked it into her pocket. She'd planned to read another that night, but that was all she could take.

She joined her own three soul mates in bed and swore they wouldn't lose touch like her mother had with hers.

• • •

Best friend Sippi's papa was coming. He had some kind of drop-off in Indianapolis, and he was going to swing by and pick up his little girl. Sue had to work hard not to hate him just as much as she hated her own father. She hadn't ever met him. She had no right, and she knew that. But he'd allowed his only daughter to be used like a plaything, and Sue couldn't reconcile that. If he was such a good papa, he would've noticed something like that.

Sippi was bouncing off the walls, grinning and spinning with joy, but slower than usual. Sue couldn't burst her bubble with negativity, so she pretended to be excited, too.

Another thing was worrying her. That morning, Sue had noticed Ms. Pearline's concern about high blood pressure. She'd set the timer to ring every sixty minutes to check Sippi's pressure. It was steadily rising, and Sue wondered if she needed to leave the apartment at all. Even walking to and from the bathroom spiked her pressure. Ms. Pearline didn't like it, that much was obvious, and neither did Sue.

"Oh, best friend Sue!" Sippi attempted to spring forward, throwing an awkward belly hug onto Sue. "I can't wait for you to meet Papa. He's such a good papa!"

"Oh, I know. Me too. How are you feeling?"

"Why does everybody keep asking me that? I'm doing just fine. Right as rain."

The timer went off again, and Sue watched as Sippi moped over to the blood pressure cuff.

"Getting dreary out," Mary drawled. "Storm's coming."

"I feel it in my bones," added Lillian.

The apartment was so high in the clouds that it felt like they were a part of the approaching storm. Sue had a horrible feeling. A dread came over her, and it wouldn't let her go. She pulled Mary and Lillian into a close circle as Ms. Pearline took Sippi's pressure.

"Is this really a good idea?" Sue asked them. "Letting her go off in a storm. She's obviously not well."

"What can we do, Sue?" Lillian snapped with an eye roll. "Her papa's coming. We have no say in the matter."

Sue looked to Mary for support. "I agree with you, Sue! Don't scowl at me. But Lillian's right. What can we do? He's blood."

Lillian grabbed hold of Sue's chin and turned it toward Sippi. "Look at that girl. Have you seen her happier than that?"

Sue really looked at her. Lillian was right. She could hardly contain her excitement to see her father.

"We can't take that from her," said Lillian. "I say we

support her in it. Love on her and be happy that she has something to smile for."

"And pray about the rest," added Mary.

"Amen."

• • •

Sue zipped herself up and put on phony excitement for Sippi's sake. Still, she noticed Sippi's blood pressure creeping up. Last time she'd taken it, Ms. Pearline told Sippi if it rose, even one more digit, she couldn't go. They all held their breath, crossed their fingers, and pretended to wish it didn't go up any farther. Sue wished it would, but it didn't. Then they cheered when Ms. Pearline gave the all clear.

There was a knock on the door. Sippi went to open it, but Tim Reese's voice was on the other side, not her father's. Sue grabbed the neck of her guitar and ran into Ms. Pearline's bedroom to hide along with the rest of them. When she got there, Sue made sure she secured the hundred-dollar bill in her sweaty palm.

He sounded even more demanding and drunk than the last time he'd visited the apartment. Charm and flattery weren't working on him now. He wasn't going to leave until he got what he came for, Sue thought. Whatever that was.

"How many girls you got back there?" he said, so sloppy that it was hard to make out. "Let me see them."

Ms. Pearline softened her tone the way she always had with Tim Reese, but he wasn't having any of it. Sue half expected him to push past Ms. Pearline and burst through the bedroom door. Then another male voice interrupted their dispute.

"Papa," Missippi whispered to Sue. "He's saving us."

Sue held a cautious finger to her mouth and shook her head, but Missippi was too excited to care. Sue wondered why Sippi didn't bound through the door to see her father like she'd expected. Instead, she hung back, grinning with her ear pressed to the door like she was waiting for something to happen.

"Who was that man?" Sue heard him ask Ms. Pearline about Tim Reese. "Didn't give off nothing nice."

Good eye, Sue thought. At least he could spot an asshole for once in his life. Because he surely missed the one in his own family. Then Sippi's father offered to give Tim Reese what he called a firm talking-to, and Sue found herself fond of him all of a sudden. She liked his thick drawl and how observant he was. Maybe it's harder to see the evils within one's family, Sue thought, trying very hard to give him the benefit of the doubt.

"That means a lot, really," Ms. Pearline told him. "but

he'll just come back as soon as you head out. I'm taking care of him."

"My only child is here with you, Ms. Pearline," he said firmly. "And my grandbaby, too. I wouldn't be doing it for you."

Sue felt her lips part. Sippi hadn't told him she was having twins. That was a huge detail to leave out, especially being this close to full term. He would likely be the one to care for them financially. Sue reached for her guitar, just in case he made a scene or got angry that she hadn't told him. She'd bash her favorite instrument over his head if he dared mess with best friend Sippi. Father or fucking not.

"Missippi is perfectly safe here, sir. I assure you." Sue was proud of Ms. Pearline's confident tone. "I take the life and health of these young ladies seriously. I would gladly lay down my own for them without as much as a blink. Also, sir . . ." Then she softened. "I thought Missippi would have told you. You have more than one grandchild coming. She's having twins."

He fell silent. Sue shook Sippi's shoulder to steel her for his wrath. Lillian pressed her ear closer to the door to listen.

"Two babies?"

"Two babies." Ms. Pearline repeated his words. "That's

right. She's high risk, so I've been paying close attention to her breathing and movement. While I'm thinking of it, I have an important question to ask you. Does Missippi ever embellish the truth about her own health? For instance, ever say she's fine when she's obviously not."

Sue would've thought it a strange question to ask, but lately, she'd wondered the same thing. Every now and then, she'd catch best friend Sippi in a wince and ask if she was okay. She always said she was. According to Sippi, she was having the easiest, least complicated, most painless pregnancy. But Sue hurt all over her body. Even her hair hurt. Deep down, she couldn't wrap her mind around two babies being easier than one baby.

"Missippi has never told me a story," he said, with such surety. "If she don't want me to know, she won't tell it, but she won't tell a bold-faced lie."

"Not even a little white one to protect you?"

"Maybe," he said. "I don't know. What is this you gave me here? I think your tea has gone bad."

Sue smiled, realizing that best friend Sippi had been waiting for her father to drink the tea. Sue watched her leap toward him.

"My God." He looked at her like a league of ghosts had entered the room, and then he started crying.

Sue realized she'd pegged him all wrong. He was a

sensitive man paddling in a river of tears. He loved his little girl and however many babies grew in her body. She wanted very much to play him a song, but she didn't know if that might come off as melodramatic. So she stood there beside Lillian and Mary and watched the large father break into tiny bits.

"Who did this to you, baby?"

"Come on, girls," Sue said. She didn't feel they should be privy to such raw family emotion, especially from a father. "Let's give them some privacy."

Then Missippi began to cry. "Wait. Papa, this is best friend Sue. And other best friends, Mary and Lillian. And you know Ms. Pearline already. They been God's gifts to my life. Oh! And the Midnight Boys coming along before too long!" She ran over to the window. "They must be sleep now, though."

"Who did this to you?"

Sue wanted to tell him that it was Sippi's uncle. Her disgusting, sorry-excuse-for-a-human-being of an uncle. She knew it wasn't her place. Missippi would never speak to her again if she did it. Still, Sue weighed it in her mind. Should she tell him and protect Sippi? Or should she protect the friendship? She was caught between two large, immovable rocks, and she had no idea which to choose.

"Papa, you a broken record now!" Missippi said to him. "Here! Listen to best friend Sue play this Johnny Cash–man song. You know him, Papa?"

"I know him. He's playing in my rig right now."

"How did you not tell me about Johnny Cash?" Missippi folded her arms. She looked so very young when she did that. Like a ten-year-old throwing a tantrum. "His songs are stories. Fun ones! That man's been everywhere! Just like you, Papa."

"Sorry, ladies," he said, smiling. "I just ain't expect . . ."

"She's carrying twins." Ms. Pearline spoke softly. "And she's carrying them right out front. Soon as she has them, her little body will go right back to where it was before. Of this I have no doubt."

"See, Papa? Ms. Pearline is smart as a whip, and if she says I'll go right back to where I was before, it's right."

"Well, then, Ms. Pearline," he said before wiping his face with his sleeve. "Is it safe to take my girl out to get some ice cream?"

"Oh, please, please, please," Missippi said. "I only been out a few times and never past the playground. Can I?"

Ms. Pearline nodded and told her father, "If you notice any shortness of breath or swelling in the ankles, bring her right back here. Also . . ." Ms. Pearline grabbed his fingers and placed them above Missippi's collarbone, instructing him to manually count her pulse.

"Okay," she said. "See how slowly you're counting? If you feel yourself counting faster than that, bring her right back. I want you to do that at least every thirty minutes. Got it?"

Missippi's papa nodded.

•••

They'd been gone for a little over an hour.

"Are we sure it was a good idea to let them go?" Sue paced loops around the bed. "They've been gone a really long time."

"I was just wondering the same, Sue." Ms. Pearline stood vigil by the window, watching intently for them to turn the corner by the playground. She bit a rip of skin from her finger and said, "I think I made a mistake."

"Ladies!" said Lillian with a huff. "Calm down—my God! You two could worry the warts off a worrywart."

"Besides," Mary added. "That's her daddy. He's got the final say in what happens to his girl."

"I have a bad feeling about this whole thing." Sue plopped down on the made bed, began nervously strumming at her guitar, and then realized she had one more letter to read.

Dear Susan,

I spoke with your horrible boyfriend again today. He came by without his parents this time, but dear Lord, he had his grandmother in tow.

Have you met her, darling? If not, she is a wonder. Smaller than a prepubescent teenage girl, but as fiery as a spinning devil. Her words carry venom inside them, and her jewels nearly blinded me when I opened the door to her. The woman didn't request admission. She marched in and sat on your father's chair. I daresay, I would admire her boldness if it weren't on such display in my own home.

She, too, as you may have guessed, came with a set of demands. She forbids adoption of her bloodline. Do prepare yourself for these:

- First, she wishes you to marry Michael.

- Second, she wishes you shut your mouth, much like your mother. (HER WORDS!)

- Third, she would like to adjust your hair and wardrobe.

- Lastly, she would like to grant you a large home in Kenilsworth, fully equipped with a maid and nurse for the baby.

She then turned to her grandson and told him that he was done with his education. He would promptly join his father's company as an apprentice. For he will, one day, take over as chairman, and you will have the "privilege" of standing by his side.

I laughed at her list, darling. She did not like that one bit.

This must be overwhelming. But I have to add more. This may be the hardest addition. Steel yourself, please.

She called your father. He knows everything, and he, from DC no less, agreed with her. He has given his blessing to this horrible family to take your hand.

I am sorry.

I love you and I am trying to find my words.

Your loving mother,

Margaret Claire Laura Hurley-Day

A pounding at the door startled the shouting voices in her head. It had to be Tim Reese. The girls scattered to the bedroom, and Ms. Pearline straightened and walked to the door. "Coming," she said.

Ms. Pearline opened the door. "Oh my God. Here, here, lay her down here."

It wasn't Tim Reese. It was best friend Sippi, looking like she was about to birth two babies within minutes. Breathing and panting and throwing her head back without even realizing it.

All voices in the room became a jumble of pitches—low, high, medium vibrations. No coherent words formed sentences. In Sue's mind, all she could see was Sippi slipping in and out of consciousness. Eyes rolling into the back of her head like broken Magic 8 Balls. She looked sickly and drawn up. Thunder crashed outside, and Sue caught sight of a few passersby running down the sidewalk.

"Chicken timer," said Ms. Pearline. "Sue . . . chicken . . . timer."

She stood and went to get it. It wasn't there. She saw the sink and the dish rags and the soap and the stacks of dishes and the Pine-Sol. She saw nothing that looked remotely like a chicken timer. It couldn't have been there. Ms. Pearline had gotten it wrong.

"Calm down, Susan," Ms. Pearline said. "Breathe. It's directly in front of you. Next to the pepper grinder. Grab it, and come to Missippi's side."

How could it have been right there the whole time? She swore she looked a few seconds ago and hadn't seen it. She picked it up and went to them. She slowly made her way through Ms. Pearline's instructions and did as she was told, trying not to focus on everything that could go wrong with her precious best friend. Twins were dangerous. Why couldn't Sue have had the twins instead of Sippi? Sue's body was more developed. Thicker and more substantial. She could handle twins. Those two babies could break poor tiny Sippi in half.

"What should I do, ma'am?" asked Sippi's father.

Best friend Sippi's father's voice broke Sue's trance. He was so scared and shaken that Sue wanted to hug him.

"That's for you and your daughter to decide. You can wait back in my bedroom or you can hold her hand while she brings these babies into the world."

Sue watched him look into his little girl's eyes. For the first time, she realized Sippi was lucky to have a father like that. A treasure of a father. A sweet, though maybe naive, father who didn't always know what to do or how to do it. But a father who tried. Sue realized that she herself wished she had a father like him.

"Sippi," he said. "My sweet baby girl."

"Papa." Sippi could barely get his name out through the thick pain.

"I'd like to stay here with you."

"You're such a good papa."

Sue, and everyone else except Ms. Pearline, cried. They all wanted fathers like that.

OLA

She just knew what she wanted—a husband and a few babies, clean bobby socks, and a white picket fence. That's it. She got through school and church and Bible study by the skin of her teeth, so she could grow up and get married.

What about that made her stupid? Nothing, that's what.

She didn't worry about much of that anymore, though. It didn't hurt her feelings. All of that stupid talk. Nothing hurt after she took Mrs. Mac's elixir. She'd floated up and up to places that felt nice. Slipping away quick and painless.

Mrs. Mac had told her to take a little every day, not the whole bottle. Soon as she drank it, she knew it was the Three Sixes that did her in. One teaspoon of that stuff could break up all the phlegm in the back of the throat after a bad cold. A whole bottle could kill.

Ola didn't know if she wanted to be dead when she drank it all. She just knew she didn't want to be a burden to Walter, and Evangelist, and most of all, to Izella.

IZELLA

Ola and her baby boy died in the ambulance on the way to the hospital while Izella scrubbed the burnt-up jowl bacon from the bottom of Mr. Melvin's stove.

MISSIPPI

Papa stayed up by Missippi's head at first. Even through the pain, she worried over him. He looked like he was about to explode right there in Ms. Pearline's apartment. Ms. Pearline said to breathe in, and he did. Ms. Pearline said to breathe out, and he did. Missippi wanted so badly to laugh at him, huffing and carrying on, but it hurt too much to laugh. Best friend Sue held the chicken timer like Missippi had during Ruby's birthing. Lillian and Mary squeezed tight on the stick between her teeth.

"I need you to control your breathing, Mississippi." Ms. Pearline was still angry. Not nervous or jittery or smiley. She was following the motions of bringing babies into the world. "Mississippi, listen to me. Breathe when I tell you to breathe. Control it!"

"I'm . . . so. . . . sorry." Missippi hated when anyone she loved was angry at her. If she hadn't been lying there on that bed about to have babies, she would've jumped up and cooked something to show how sorry she truly was.

"Everyone out," said Ms. Pearline. "Now!"

The room fell silent except for the ticking of Sue's chicken timer. "What?" asked Sue. "She's probably really close . . ."

"I said," said Ms. Pearline in an angrier voice than Sippi'd ever heard from her, "out!"

Everyone else scattered, and the room quieted, leaving Missippi gap-legged on the bed with Ms. Pearline on her knees between Missippi's.

"Mississippi." Ms. Pearline lifted into a squat but never left her place. "I need you to listen carefully to what I am about to say. We don't have much time. I am not angry at you. I am concerned for the safety of your babies, one of which is semi-breeched. You are not following the instructions I'm giving you closely enough. Do you understand what I'm telling you?"

Missippi nodded in response. "I thought you hated me," she said between intense contractions.

"I love you, child." Ms. Pearline squeezed a smile out through her fear. "I just need you to do everything I say. It's very important. Life-and-death important. Okay?"

When Missippi nodded again, Ms. Pearline permitted everyone to go back to their places.

"We're entering the transition phase," Ms. Pearline announced. "The end is in sight. Sippi, would you like to go to the tub or stay here?"

Missippi was so glad to hear Ms. Pearline call her Sippi. She looked around her. Walls covered with pretty pictures painted by other girls with swollen bellies. Mary and Lillian smiling down on either side. Best friend Sue rubbing her leg and ticking the timer. And Papa. Telling her that everything was going to be okay in his thick Valdosta twang.

"I'm happy here."

"Okay. The contractions will come every thirty to ninety seconds now, and they can last up to two minutes. Sippi, this means you'll have little time to recover between them. If it gets too much, we'll go to the tub. Here comes one now. Breathe."

The whole world shrunk into a thing of pain. Long, hard pain with no relief to look forward to. The intense urge to push came over Missippi. Her stomach pounded loud and mean as a twister, and her body told her she needed to empty it.

"No!" yelled Ms. Pearline. "You are not ready to push. Do not push, you hear me? Stop! Pushing!"

"What's wrong?" asked Papa. "Dear God, Pearline, what is it?"

"She cannot push until she's fully dilated. I know you want to push now, Sippi, but I need you to control it. Control your little body. Short mini breaths now. Show me your pant, come on, baby. Tongue out and everything."

The urge was stronger than anything ever before in her life. It would feel so much better if she gave in to it. Ms. Pearline told her to pant and hold whatever it was on the inside, but her body couldn't stop.

"I can't stop it." Missippi squeezed her butt cheeks together and tried and tried to stop it. Her body was taking over.

"You need to calm down, Sippi," said Ms. Pearline. "You're in a panic. I need you to think of calm, short breaths. Look, we'll all do it with you."

Lillian started panting like a hot dog, and Mary joined her. Best friend Sue put down the timer and started playing soft, slow tunes on her guitar. Ms. Pearline watched for Missippi's babies, making sure they hadn't crowned before they were ready. Then there was Papa.

"Did I ever tell you about the time your mama came home barefoot in the wintertime?" He was smiling. As calm as the first breeze of spring. "Valdosta winter ain't but fifty degrees, but still. She had the whole neighborhood fussing over her that day. Everybody loved your mama, Sippi-girl. But nobody as much as me. She was my light. I used to call her that. Not baby or honey or sweetheart. No, ma'am. She was my bright, bright light.

"She'd given her shoes away to another mama down the road from us. A mama that couldn't afford to get her own shoes for her own feet in the wintertime. We didn't have much of nothing, but if she had a quarter, she give away a dime of it without a second thought.

"I wish you could've had time to know her, Sippi."

The urge to push calmed. The panic attack let up. Papa had never spoken of her mother. Not that she could remember at least, and she'd long given up on asking. He stared off for a while. Quiet. Rapt. Fixed on his own memory.

"But I tell you what," he said. "Your babies are gonna

know you. You understand me? They gonna know how wonderful you are, girl. You just got to breathe like Ms. Pearline tells you to breathe, and they gonna know you. You hear?"

Sippi reached up to his face. "Such a good papa."

• • •

Missippi named them Author and Easy. A baby boy and a baby girl, just like she'd known all along. Their cries sounded like the wind chimes from her dreams. Bells, tiny, sweet bells ringing to let everyone know they were there and healthy.

• • •

The twins slept through the night. Not like Ruby's baby boy, who hollered like a siren no matter what. Author and Easy were dream babies, Ms. Pearline had called them.

The sun peeked over the high-rises of downtown Chicago, and a familiar pounding sounded off—Tim Reese. The babies screamed at the disruption, and no amount of rocking would quiet them down. It was as if they sensed a mean man coming.

"I hear them little heathens!" he yelled, clearly drunk. "Let me in now, woman, or I'll break it down!"

Papa leaped up and went to the door. "Everybody

lock up in the bathroom. Deadbolt it behind you. Sippi and the babies in the tub."

"I'm staying right here with you," said Sippi, barely able to stand.

"Get in there, girl!"

"Come on, best friend," said Sue. "Babies need you with them."

Missippi went with her into the small bathroom. They couldn't hear as well from there. Only muffled sounds of men arguing back and forth and random neighbors inspecting the ruckus from their apartments.

After a loud crash, Ms. Pearline went into the living room with them and began demanding Mr. Reese leave.

He finally did.

The girls came out of the bathroom to find Ms. Pearline holding a bloody rag over Papa's forehead. The coffee table was shattered, and a crowd of neighbors had gathered at the open door. The babies had both stopped crying, and they stared at Missippi with big, beautiful, innocent eyes.

"Sippi," Papa started. "Gather your things. I'm taking you home."

Sue shouted, "You can't." Terrified tears running down her face. "You just can't."

Missippi wanted to protest. Wanted to agree with

her sweet best friend Sue. But since the babies had come into the world hours earlier, something had shifted in her body. It wasn't about what she wanted anymore. Nothing she desired mattered, not one little bit. She just had to protect them. She couldn't stay.

"I have to go, best friend."

"Fine, then," said Sue. "I'm coming with you."

SUE

Sue packed her guitar and a single bag to join Sippi and her papa. Ms. Pearline went to the neighbor's apartment to call Sue's mother to inform her that Sue was leaving. Ms. Pearline wasn't angry at all. Sue had expected her to be angry, but she seemed resolved. Accepting it as Sue's choice and not her own. As she hung up the phone, Ms. Pearline removed the coverings from her own body and began wrapping Sue's neck and face in her scarf and blanket.

"You two need to head out before rush hour," Ms. Pearline said with heavy sadness. "We don't want anyone to catch you. You're an odd couple for this neighborhood."

"What did my mother say?" Sue asked Ms. Pearline while being wrapped like a tick.

"She said to call her as soon as you get to Valdosta," Ms. Pearline replied with cracks in her voice. "And that she loves you, darling. Her words."

Lillian and Mary began to cry openly, but they didn't object. They knew it was the right thing. Sippi handed Author to Lillian and Easy to Mary for them to cuddle for the last time. The move instantly dried their tears and turned their faces into smiles. Those two children were the cure for sadness.

"I think I have everything," said Sippi.

"Me too. Am I wrapped enough?" Sue asked Ms. Pearline.

Ms. Pearline nodded nervously and lowered her gaze. She must've been exhausted, just delivering two babies the night before. And then dealing with horrible Tim Reese that morning. She was an unbelievable woman.

"Thank you for everything you've done." Sue looked from her to the twins to Sippi. "Everything. For Margaret, too."

Ms. Pearline bowed her head in acknowledgment.

Missippi walked to her with her arms wide and brought her in tight for the hug that broke something in Ms. Pearline. Her barriers opened. She wailed and wailed before saying, "I'll miss you, Missippi. I'll miss you the most."

The room watched as they painfully said good-bye.

And then the five of them left—Missippi holding her twins, followed by her papa, and then Sue.

The giant rig was backed right up to the entrance of the apartment so no one saw them. He'd laid down an entire floor of blue painting blankets in the back and nailed down two small boxes filled with knitted blankets for the babies. Sippi stepped in first, wincing at the movement. Then Papa rolled down the back door.

He revved the enormous engine, and they were off. The first hour of the ride was Chicago's nauseating stop-and-go traffic. Everything in the rear of the truck shifted and stopped over and over until Sue wanted to vomit. The small, battery-powered light near the cab was just enough to illuminate her best friend and the beautiful new babies she'd just brought into the world. Sippi looked exhausted.

"How are you feeling?" Instead of focusing on her own stomachache, Sue decided to ask about Sippi. She had, after all, just had not one, but two babies. "Tell me the truth or I'll know."

Sippi forced a smile in response. "I feel on cloud nine with these little angels. But my body feels like it's been run over. Specially . . ." She lowered her voice to a whisper. "Down there. It hurts, best friend. It hurts real bad."

For Sippi's sake, Sue didn't want to push too hard for information. But for her own sake, she wanted to know. Her own baby was coming in a few months, and she had no idea what to expect.

Sue decided to ask her. "Tell me what it feels like."

Sippi didn't seem upset. Actually, she seemed kind of excited to know something Sue didn't know.

"Well . . ." She leaned in. "You ever been punched in the cheekbone before?"

"Of course not, have you?"

"I have," Sippi replied. "Well, kicked actually. But not by a person, by a mule. On my cousin's farm, he bucked me square in the cheek. Now, I've been hit before, but there's something special and horrible about a cheek hit. It's dull and aching. It hurts all day and all night. That's what I feel like . . . down there. Like a hard punch in the cheek."

"I don't get it," Sue replied honestly.

"I know. It's hard to say out loud how something feels on the inside. Here, give me your arm." Sippi held her hand out, grabbed Sue's thin left upper arm, and punched it.

"Ouch!" Sue snatched it back.

"No, no, wait. You're going to lose it. Look," Sippi

said, staring at the spot she'd punched Sue. "I punched a frog out."

Sue saw it just before it went down. A golf-ball-size lump in her skin, peeking up and then back down.

"Did you catch how it felt a little bit dull and made your arm sleepy?"

Sue nodded.

"That's how I'm feeling," Sippi said. "Only a million times worse."

Sue thought about that. Dull, aching pain in the vagina. She'd never thought much about having a vagina at all, really. Vaginas are hidden. Used only when necessary for pleasure and pee, but never seen. Boys, on the other hand, named their penises. Horrible Michael called his Teddy, after the "Chappaquiddick Incident" Kennedy. Sue hated him.

She hadn't had adequate time to think about him showing up at her home like that. Threatening the nightmare of Kenilworth aristocratic marriage on her. Housewifery. She would never do it. His grandmama couldn't make her. Her father could never make her. What were they going to do? Tie her down? Make her say her vows to a phony? Never.

"What's on your mind?" Best friend Sippi interrupted her thoughts. "Did I scare you?"

"Nothing. Just can't believe these babies are so quiet and calm. You're a lucky girl. I hope I'm that lucky."

"So you've decided to keep yours?" Sippi smiled like a girl much older than fourteen. She didn't bounce at all. Sue couldn't tell if it hurt, or if giving birth had taken her best friend Sippi's bounce away forever.

"I don't know," Sue said honestly. "I'm scared to even think of it."

"Are you having a little girl or a little boy?" Sippi asked, again with a more mature countenance. Sue didn't know how to answer her question. "I mean, when it speaks to you. Is it a little boy or a little girl?"

Sue sat quiet for a few seconds, listening for a little voice to help her answer the question. She felt a bit embarrassed that she'd never even tried to talk to it. Maybe that made her less motherly or something. Not woman enough to be a mother, not that she wanted to be one necessarily.

"I haven't heard anything from it."

"That's okay, best friend." Sippi closed her exhausted eyes. "You should sing to it sometime. It might sing with you."

Four hours into the ride to Valdosta and only Easy had woken up to nurse. Sippi fell asleep with the little one on her nipple, and Sue maneuvered her out of Sippi's arms. She rocked the smiling baby back and forth as they walked the length of the rig's cabin. Only the small light in the corner guided her through the darkness, but Sue could tell Sippi's papa did all he could to make it comfortable for them. Wooden shelves had been cleared of their boxes and other contents. A wicker basket filled to the brim with room-temperature Cokes and salt-and-vinegar potato chips hung on a hook near the cab, and stacks of blue blankets covered the cold metal floor. He'd done his best, Sue knew. He really was a good papa, just like Sippi had been telling her all along.

"Hey, little buddy," Sue kept saying to Easy. "Hey there."

Sue hadn't realized babies that young knew how to smile and coo. She was a dream of a little human being, and Sue felt privileged to hold her. She'd never actually held a baby before. Her aunt tried to make her hold hers. Sue never did. She'd always been scared to break or drop them. But these two babies were an extension of her best friend. They were more family than any cousin could ever be.

Sue began singing and swaying as Easy dozed off in her arms.

"I fell into a burning ring of fire. I went down, down, down, and the flames went higher . . ."

And then she heard it—a little girl's voice singing along from inside her.

A girl.

• • •

They arrived in Valdosta on a Tuesday. Sippi's papa pulled up to the back door, and there they were in the driveway of a skinny house. Sue's neighbors back in Kenilworth had bathrooms larger than best friend Sippi's entire home. She felt a jolt of guilt shoot through her. Why did she deserve such privilege when sweet, innocent Sippi and brave, beautiful Ms. Pearline lived with so little? She didn't want to show it on her face. She smiled a bit too big, like a sad clown putting on a show. Sue noticed a few people gawking at her; all of them wore head-to-toe black in hundred-degree heat. Some even wore small veils on their heads. To Sue, it looked like a town in mourning.

"What's going on, Papa?" Sippi had noticed it, too.

"Y'all go on inside and pour up some sweet tea while I ask Mr. Turner next door what's what."

Sippi wrapped Author in his blanket and handed him to Sue, while she carried Easy. Through it all, they slept soundly.

The small living room was clean and quaint, but it

was as hot as the outside. Scorching hot. Beads of sweat gathered around Author's sleeping little nose, and Sue wiped them away with her sleeve. She, too, was sweating. Her blond hair stuck to the nape of her neck, and her shirt became drenched quickly.

"I'll turn on the fan," said Sippi. "I don't even feel it anymore. See?" She wiped her face. "Sweat-free. Let's put the babies down in my bed."

When they went back into the kitchen afterward to make tea, Sippi's papa walked through the door looking alarmed.

"What's wrong, Papa?"

He took his hat off before speaking. "It's Ola. Pretty gal from down the way, just about your age, Sue. She died yesterday with a baby inside her."

Sippi fell backward onto the checkerboard kitchen floor. Sue couldn't tell if she'd actually fainted or just fell. But she watched helplessly as her best friend lost all control over her little legs.

• • •

Sippi slept and cried all day while Sue and Papa watched over the babies. Sippi needed sleep. She'd been tired from labor and had hardly slept on the ride down to Georgia.

While Sippi slept, Sue called her mother to check in.

Her mother sounded worried, and happy to hear that her daughter had arrived safely. Sue's mother then asked to speak with Sippi's papa, probably to thank him and offer compensation for her daughter's care. Sue heard him refuse outright and thank her for the kind offer.

She was flying in tomorrow morning to bring Sue back to Kenilworth. Sue daydreamed of bringing Sippi and the babies back with them. They surely had the room in their large, lonely home. But it was impossible, Sue thought. There was not a single family like best friend Sippi's anywhere near her. They lived on the opposite side of her town. Sue'd never really thought about that until that moment. Everyone she knew back home looked exactly like her. Everyone.

"Do you know who did this to my baby girl?" Sippi's papa asked Sue out the blue. "She won't tell me."

"I do," Sue replied honestly, biting her tongue not to let it slip. Sippi would never forgive that level of betrayal. "But I can't say."

"Please," he pleaded, looking like a man with a broken heart and racked brain. "I've been trying to narrow it down to who. I can't see it, Sue. Please. I can't see it."

He deserved to know more than anyone. Certainly more than Sue. He was, after all, her papa. A good one, too.

"If I tell you, she'll never speak to me again."

"If you don't tell me, he could do this to her again."

It was the right response. He was absolutely right. Breaking this promise was justifiable. This wasn't a secret told behind a locker at school about a boy she liked. This was life and death. With innocent best friend Sippi in the crosshairs. Sippi didn't know. She was a child. Fourteen. A young fourteen at that. Sue visualized a man overtop of her young body. Sex could be the most beautiful thing in the world. But it could also be more tragic than death. More painful than any other agony on earth.

Sippi's papa slid off the couch and onto his knees, pleading. Crying. Holding his head in his large hands. He could do anything he wanted with those hands, Sue thought. He could build anything. Drive anything. Lift anything, no matter how heavy. But he couldn't protect his only child, because he didn't know who to protect her from.

Sue thought of Sippi. She was back in Valdosta, where the devil lived. He was here somewhere, lurking and waiting for her papa's rig to back out the drive. He could be watching right now. Waiting to hold the tiny babies he'd forced inside her best friend. Author and Easy.

"It was her uncle," Sue blurted angrily. "She calls him Unc."

• • •

The next morning, Sue woke up to Author and Easy screaming, and Sippi's papa gone. Sippi sat in her rocking chair, wearing head-to-toe black just like everyone else.

"Hadn't slept that long in years," Sippi said to Sue. "Thank you for watching them."

Sue wiped her face with her hands and gave the pillow one last squeeze before lifting herself from Sippi's bed. "I love them," she said. "I don't mind it."

Sippi locked eyes with Sue. "Y'all have godparents where you come from?"

"I'm not Catholic."

"Me, neither."

Then Sue realized what Sippi was saying to her. "Oh, Sippi."

"Is that a yes?"

"That's a yes."

Sippi got up from the rocking chair and placed the babies on the foot of the bed. She then brought the brown Bible and hovered over their heads. "I don't know what words to say. Um . . . I'll say that I love you, best friend Sue. You've been a gift to me. Brought in straight from God. Who would've thought it?" Sippi smiled and let a single tear fall from her eye. "I don't mean to cry. I'm cried out. I mean to smile and laugh and let these two young'uns know that they couldn't ask for a better godmama. And I couldn't ask for a better best friend."

Sue looked from Sippi to the babies. She wanted to hug them, but all she could think of was her own betrayal.

"Sippi . . ." Sue started to tell her the truth. "I need to tell you."

"Hold on," Sippi interrupted. She slowly walked over to the small window and pulled a bottle of warm olive oil from the sill. "Blessed oil."

Sippi opened the tight lid and stood over Sue. "You promise to look out for Author and Easy when you can?"

Sue felt the heaviness of the moment, weighing down on her. "I do."

Sippi drew an oily cross on her forehead. Then, with the same slick finger, drew tiny crosses on Author's and Easy's, too. "Done. I'll go make some us some two-step biscuits to celebrate."

• • •

Sue's mother showed up before Sippi's father returned.

Within seconds, Margaret grabbed ahold of Easy and would not let her go. Deep down, Sue was afraid of how her mother would fit in the tiny living room. Demure and statuesque by nature, she could come across as a snob, and

Sue didn't want that. But as soon as Margaret crossed the threshold, she belonged there.

Sue had never seen anything like that before. Her mother dropped every ounce of the Vineyard from her voice and slouched her shoulders, relaxed. She wore a basic white T-shirt and jeans. Sue hadn't realized her mother owned a pair of jeans. Her hair was tied up in a messy bun, and only a small dash of pink stained her bottom lip. No more makeup than that.

But it was watching her with Easy that Sue would never forget. They were instant soul mates. Laughing together. Sue's mother kept making funny faces at her, and Easy stared back, seemingly mesmerized. When Author reached for them, Sue's mother held them both, one on each thigh. He, too, smiled, but Easy looked to be fixated on her.

"She loves you already, Miss Margaret," Sippi said, watching her with her daughter.

"Oh please, darling. Call me Maggie."

Maggie. Sue felt her jaw drop. Maggie.

"I'll call you Miss Maggie," Sippi said, grinning. "Down south, our elders are miss and mister whether they want to be or not. Would you like a two-step biscuit?"

"Well, I don't know what that is, but I'd love to try one."

"Tea, too?"

"I'd absolutely love tea, thank you."

Sue laughed under her breath at their different interpretations of tea. To best friend Sippi, tea was freezing cold and as sweet as a dessert. To Mother, it was as hot as Valdosta and bitter, with a touch of lemon. She was about to be unpleasantly surprised.

"Darling," Margaret said as Sippi turned into the kitchen. "Our flight will be leaving soon. Gather your things. We cannot miss it."

Sue's stomach turned at the thought of leaving Author and Easy. "But can't we take the first flight out tomorrow? I couldn't leave her alone like this. Not with the babies all by herself."

"Dear," Margaret started, trying to choose her words carefully. "I want that." She glanced down at Author and Easy, now resting quietly on her knees. "More than you know. But it's your father, darling. He will come here if we do not make our flight. And he is not as . . . amiable as I am. I am sorry."

Sue couldn't say anything. There was no arguing with reality.

"Would you hold them while I go help in the kitchen, darling?"

Margaret placed the babies in Sue's arms. "They are dreams, aren't they?"

"They are," Sue replied, staring at her godchildren. They still had greasy crosses drawn on their little foreheads, and they looked to her with such love and longing.

"I'll send in Mississippi to sit with you."

When her mother left the room, Sippi returned. Sue sang to Author, Easy, and best friend Sippi until it was time to leave.

IZELLA

Everyone wore black.

Ola hated black.

She preferred color.

They didn't know Ola at all. They wore black because Valdosta told them to wear black, not because they loved Ola.

The funeral was tomorrow. It was probably going to get rained out and muddy at the grave site. Izella hoped the already-dug grave would fill up with rain-water so Ola couldn't fit in there. It was a childish thing to think—Izella knew that. But when she closed her eyes, she saw it. Too full to fit a casket. Funeral canceled.

Mr. Melvin kept checking on her. It must've taken all of his energy to get up and walk down the hall over and over. He was a nice man.

Evangelist stayed busy. Weeds had taken over the tomato plants, and Evangelist got bit up by mosquitoes from pulling them all day long. She went out there and only came in to pee.

Izella had never seen so much food in her life. Barrels of collards, tubs of squash, countertop covered up with roasts and chickens. Pans and pans of dressing in the oven and macaroni boiling on all four eyes. Izella cooked it all. She didn't want to go anywhere near her bedroom. She'd only gone in there to open up a window to air it out. It still smelled too much like Ola.

Izella took to the cooking like a fish to water. No one to tell her she was too young to work the big knives or hot pans. Evangelist let her loose, checking in every now and then, but obsessively pulling weeds all day. Izella longed for the day they all stood around the sink, cleaning and separating vegetables for the deep freeze—her, Evangelist, and her sister.

"You all right?" said Mr. Melvin for the thirtieth time.

"Yes," Izella snapped. "I told you yes."

• • •

Night fell on the house. And everything was cooked and labeled. Enough food to feed five hundred folks, easy. Izella opened every pantry to find something else to cook. But there was already too much food, and she knew it.

Midnight was oncoming. That meant it was about to be the day of Ola's funeral. Izella went out the back porch and jumped the fence to find Stanley Turner mixing moonshine.

"Birthday's coming," he said without acknowledging Ola's death at all.

Izella was happy he hadn't. It was all anyone had been talking about all week long. All she had been thinking about. Her birthday was never a big deal to her anyway. She'd usually forgotten it.

"Twelve days away now," he said. "Well, eleven now. Just turned midnight."

It was officially the day of Ola's funeral. She'd have to sit in the front row next to Evangelist. Within feet of Ola's stuffed body. She wasn't in there anymore. Izella wondered what they put on her dead body. Hopefully it was the blue paisley dress. That'd been her favorite one.

"You got a sip of that stuff you always want me to try?" Izella asked, needing something to help her along.

"Not today, I don't," Stanley said with resolve. "Days like today ain't for forgetting. Days like today are for remembering."

Izella took a seat at his side. He was eaten up by mosquitoes just like Evangelist. Not even bothering to slap them away as they sucked his lumpy legs.

"They don't bother you?" Izella asked before smacking one from her ankle.

"They just trying to live best they know how. We all doing the same thing."

Izella didn't understand him at all. He was drunk. He had no idea what he was talking about himself, she thought. Still, she sat there and watched as he mixed and turned and heated the liquid. Finally pouring it into glass gallons.

She watched him until the sun came up.

SUE

Sue's father still wore his American-flag pin on his lapel.

"Been a few months," Sue said to her father as she entered the house.

"Susan," he said. "You know Michael's grandmother, Mrs. Blohm, I presume."

"I haven't had the pleasure."

As soon as she saw her in person, she understood what her mother had meant in the letters. Even hunched over on a walker, the woman sent chills of intimidation down Sue's spine.

"Come sit here," she said as if she owned the place. "We need to have a chat."

Michael already sat on the opposite couch with his lip poked out. Sue wanted to whack him.

There they all sat—Sue's mother and father across from Michael and his grandmother. Sue knew her future was about to be chosen for her. She wanted to be strong. She wanted to ask questions. Make waves. Challenge her future as her own.

"You will marry." Mrs. Blohm's words shook with age. "Young lady, my grandson knows this. He put up a valiant fight. He has no choice, and neither do you. You will carry on the Blohm name, and so will this child growing inside of you. What is your full name?"

"Susan Anna Day."

"Your name will be Susan Anna Day-Blohm, and you will live in a home much like this one." Mrs. Blohm looked around, seemingly judging her mother's choice of curtains. "You could do worse, child," Mrs. Blohm told her grandson. "At least they have decent taste."

Sue saw her life flash before her. Her mother's life of silent activism.

As if reading her mind, her mother smiled with pity in her eyes. She knew it, too.

Sue's life no longer revolved around sound or music

or protests anymore. Now her life revolved around a baby girl.

She would sit quietly. Sip tea. And marry a boy she hated.

But she was still Susan. And, even quietly, Susan would find a way to fight for a fucking cause.

•••

Days later, after a nightmare of a first meeting with her future grandmother-in-law, Sue walked into her room to find a framed painting of four girls holding hands. Walking away from chaos. Together.

MISSIPPI AND IZELLA

Valdosta closed down for the funeral. All corner stores, bodegas, even restaurants shut their doors for their employees to attend. Evangelist and Mr. Melvin rode along in the hearse. Izella walked to the church two hours early. She took the sidewalks and skipped the cracks, just like Ola always had. Everyone she passed wore black, but she'd refused. Instead, she wore a light blue dress and bobby socks.

Missippi watched her skip the cracks in her light blue. She'd already laid out her only black dress the night before, but when she saw Izella walking past, she knew she needed to wear color. She found a blue skirt and blue lace shirt in the back of her closet and dressed her young'uns in white. They all wore bobby socks.

•••

Izella sat alone in the church until the second person showed up. Second, third, and fourth actually. Missippi had brought her young'uns up to sit next to her on the front pew.

"Mind if we sit?" she asked. "We'll move when everybody gets here. You can say no. I won't be mad."

"Sit where you want."

Missippi sat with Izella, twins in her lap. "We saw you coming early and all alone. We wanted to come see you."

"Who is we?"

Missippi smiled. "Me and my young'uns—this is Author, and this is Easy. Boy and girl. You can tell them apart by the birthmark around her left eye."

"They ain't see me. They what, a week? You saw me. Just you."

Missippi remained silent. She didn't know what to say to that.

Izella stayed quiet, too. She shouldn't treat this girl like this. She had never met her. She didn't deserve it.

"Sorry," Izella said.

"No need."

"You wore blue." Izella noticed. "That was Ola's favorite color."

"I know that." Missippi remembered Ola in her blue striped dress. "I watched y'all walk by every day. I made up stories about y'all."

Izella was shocked to hear this. It took a lot to shock Izella. She thought she was pretty observant of her surroundings, but she'd never once seen this young girl watching them.

"I'm in that old blue house with the rig out front." Missippi realized Izella had no idea who she was.

"Why didn't you speak?" Izella asked.

Missippi shrugged. "I suppose I could've. Y'all looked perfectly fine on your own, though."

She was so right, Izella thought. They were happy with each other. Izella and Ola. Ola and Izella. They were perfect. Izella looked at the two babies. They reminded her of herself and Ola. Two siblings, forever connected. It had been her fault. Izella had made Ola go to Mrs. Mac. She'd killed her sister. Her best friend.

"Can I tell you something?" Izella asked.

"Anything in the world."

Izella turned toward Missippi. "When your babies get big enough to know what's what, keep them close, you hear? Don't think they know what they doing. They don't. They just floating through life like yellow pollen on the wind."

"I hear you," Missippi replied. "Can I tell you something, too?"

"Anything in the world."

"Sometimes you gotta let things be. Set it all loose or else you lose yourself." Missippi reached for Izella's hand. "You got folks loving you that you don't even know are there."

Izella forced herself to hold the tears back. It wasn't her way to cry.

NOW

The waiting room smelled like the first day of menstruation. The noisy air conditioner wasn't enough to dry the sweat from Tye's cheeks, still rosy with hope, but just barely. Vomit-green plastic chairs were bolted into the glossy ceramic-tile floor. The chairs were hooked together, surrounding the perimeter of a long, narrow room that was shaped like a railway car. Tye and Izella huddled around the television, staring at the blank screen as if willing it to come to life.

"Would somebody cut the TV back on?" Tye hollered at the glassed-in receptionist desk. Her freshly braided butt-length micro braids tugged at her hairline. "We deserve to know!"

"Your appointment was at four." Izella glanced at her watch. "It's coming up on six. Something's not right. I can feel it in my bones."

"I'm sorry, Gran." Tye softened her tone when speaking to her god-grandmother Izella. "Will the restaurant run all right without you?"

"Rutabaga's Diner has been up and running every day for the last thirty-seven years, Babygal." Gran Izella pinched Tye's left cheek. "Surely they can make it through one supper rush without me shouting at them what to do."

Tye sighed at the blank television. "I doubt any of us could make it through anything without you shouting at us what to do, Gran." Tye leaned her head on her gran Izella's shoulder and winced at her too-tight braids.

Izella smiled the same smile she gave Tye when Easy gave birth to her almost eighteen years earlier. "You're gonna learn, child," Gran Izella said with wisdom all over her. "Those heavy braids will rip every bit of hair from your head. I'm trying to tell you what I know, now."

"But, Gran!" Tye laughed. "You're wearing the exact same braids right now!"

They laughed loudly together, even there in the clinic

waiting room. They loved each other deeply, Tye and Izella. And nothing could separate them from each other—not age nor generation; not even Tye's own mother, Easy, could reach her like Gran Izella could. When Tye first peeked at the world through her foggy, infant eyes, she saw only Izella and hadn't dared look away since.

They watched the same movies, read the same books, and talked for hours about everything and nothing. But the main thing they had in common was they were both natural leaders. People followed them around like sheep, hanging on their words. When Tye was elected senior class president, Gran Izella made the front page of the *Atlanta Times* for Rutabaga's Diner. When Gran Izella's homemade chocolate cake earned a J. B. Culinary Award, Tye was crowned homecoming queen. They were both powerful, and that type of power was misunderstood by those without it. No one knew what it felt like to be a leader like another leader. They were soul mates.

That's why the moment Tye realized she'd missed her period, without a second thought, she called Gran Izella first. Who else would she call? Her mother would lecture her like she was one of her undergraduate English students at Emory. Her grandmother, Sippi, back in Valdosta, would just pray until her knees gave out. And her other god-grandmother, Sue, was a thousand miles away in Chicago, probably busy with some ritzy gallery opening.

Only Izella knew, and that was enough for Tye. Still, it was a betrayal, choosing Gran Izella over the rest of them. And the risk Izella herself was taking by hiding it from them was more than Tye should've ever asked of her.

They were airtight—Grandma Sippi, Gran Izella, and Nana Sue, SIS for short. Tye could never squeeze the origin story of their friendship out of them, but they were bonded together like cooled lava. No cracks or kinks, only smooth, beautiful friendship forged over time. Tye hoped for such love in her own life. Yet she was asking Gran Izella to outright lie to SIS for her sake. Regret crept into her chest, nearing her heart.

It would all be over very soon, though, Tye thought. All preliminary examinations and mandatory ultrasounds were done. Surely the Supreme Court would take more than a day to deliberate such a wide-reaching decision as abortion rights, even if the court did lean majority conservative. She would get her procedure and graduate high school next week, and her future would begin with no one the wiser.

Tye'd been accepted to Harvard, Yale, Howard, Vanderbilt, Emory, and Cal State, and she'd received numerous unsolicited offers from random schools all around the country.

Harvard's was the offer she'd accepted—full ride with a concentration in English/poetry and a thousand-dollar-per-month stipend for working at Widener Library three days a week. She worked her ass off to get that offer, and she would never be able to handle the workload with a screaming baby on her hip. Eliminating the pregnancy was her right. Her choice. Hers alone. And with Gran Izella at her flank, she could handle anything.

"Here they come," whispered Gran Izella, spotting shadowy footsteps nearing the waiting-room door. "I don't like the feel of it."

Tye lifted her chin, readying herself for anything. She didn't like the feel of it, either.

The heavy steel door leading to the examination rooms scraped open. Three nurses in pink scrubs, two receptionists, and one doctor huddled in the doorway. Their collective expressions sullen and grave with worry. The oldest-looking nurse stepped out of the clump, holding a single sheet of white paper. The nurse pushed her glasses farther up her nose and cleared her throat.

Suddenly something pelted the window behind Tye and Izella, causing them to leap from their seats. The object left a large gash and traveling cracks in the center of the dingy glass. More objects were being flung at the single waiting-room window, one after the other after the other. The nurses pulled Tye and Izella into the locked receptionist area.

"Duck down here," the older nurse whispered before pointing to the double-plated glass. "Bulletproof."

"Bulletproof?" was the only word Tye could think to say before more loud crashes seemingly rang down from all sides of the clinic.

Then, as quickly as it had started, everything went silent. Red and blue lights lit up all four walls. Thank God, Tye thought.

And then an orchestra of buzzing surrounded them—phones.

Hidden in the backs of drawers and purses and coat pockets. Some left in haste in the vomit-green chairs in the waiting room. Tye's was there among them, buzzing away across the glossy waiting-room floor and out of reach. Only the doctor had his phone in his hands.

He squeezed it alive and slowly read the screen until his face scrunched and went beet red. "I'm very sorry." He crouched down beside them. With his starched white lab coat scraping the dusty floor under the receptionist's desk, he rested the whole of his attention on Tye. "We cannot move forward with your procedure, Tyesha. Abortion is officially illegal in these United States."

The buzzing was replaced by uproarious laughter and resounding cheers from the abortion clinic parking lot.

"My God," Izella said to herself. "Not this again."

11 Weeks (the next day)

After helping with the lunch rush, Tye went into Rutabaga's stockroom to lie down. The nauseating variety of smells was getting to her—white and brown gravy, shrimp and grits, and twice-marinated steak. The strength of their stench mixed together and lifted her stomach up and down and left to right inside her body like ocean waves.

The sun was high and bright on the Atlanta afternoon, and a muted episode of *Wendy Williams* gave her the approximate time—from 3:00 to 3:22 p.m., since Hot Topics was still on. She despised Wendy Williams but still watched every day. When the commercial came, she tried to fall asleep on the small love seat, but it was no use. The smells, dear God, were overwhelming.

Another thing keeping her awake was the constant vibrations emitted from her cell phone—Twitter notifications. She watched her number of followers tick up, which brought her both joy and terror. Her original Twitter felt like an intimate coffee shop of like-minded beatniks, appreciating one another's viewpoints and perspectives and poetry. Twitter now was an enormous amount of people hanging on her every word. It was beginning to feel like an angry auditorium of eyeballs.

She'd just cracked the twenty-thousand mark, and it made her remember when she'd first opened her account. She was barely a teenager, holding court with congressmen and senators who misjudged naivete from her fresh-faced profile picture. Her first follower, a middle-aged white guy named Marc from the outskirts of New York City, defended her positions with unwavering fervor. Tye felt grateful to Marc, because he provided a middle-aged-white-guy legitimacy to her young-black-female perspective. No matter how rational and/or eloquent an argument she put forth, Marc's stamp of approval shut the mouths of millions. She was equally pissed off and accepting of that sad realization.

For a time, she shouted into the Twitter void with Marc as her strangely loyal sidekick. Then the well split open. One random Tuesday afternoon, Tye sent out the tweet heard round the world. It read as follows:

Is it me or does senator john macdonald always and I mean always have sex in his eyes? #creep

It was a nothing tweet, Tye thought. But that's usually how social-media storms work. Tye'd been throwing tiny, stinging snowballs into the elected-official Twitterverse for months, but that one kept rolling and transformed itself into an abominable snowman, large enough to take down a US senator. As it turned out, Senator John Macdonald did have sex in his eyes, a lot of sex in his eyes. Underage sex, actually.

At first, the euphoria associated with gaining followers was intoxicating. Tye, a teenager from Atlanta, Georgia, had achieved what most people her age could only dream of. She'd earned herself a captive audience of people to hang on to her words. But it all turned ugly, fast. Senator Macdonald's supporters built what can only be called a strategic and targeted attack against Tye. Thousands of negative tweets and mentions picking apart everything from her looks to her poetry, and mostly coming from adults. It was a brutal, but necessary, introduction into public life.

The most horrifying bit of political mudslinging came from Nana Sue's father, Senator Day. He personally reached out to Gran Izella. Attempting to utilize his own daughter's friendship as a breakthrough point to save his creepy friend's career. But it had only backfired. Nana Sue released a statement, condemning her horrible father and effectively hammering Senator Macdonald's political coffin shut for good.

When the senator's lackeys swarmed, Tye made a concerted effort to respond to every critique, even the ones where she was called a cunt or a bitch or a whore. She was a natural counter-puncher in such situations. Her fingers knew what to do, and she trusted her own instincts, posting public responses to some of the most vile terms in the English language. She continued, almost around the clock for twelve days, when Gran Izella noticed what she called a deep-set look on Tye.

Tye brushed her gran off, but as soon as she was alone, she looked in the mirror for the first time in days. Her cheekbones were more pronounced than usual. Her shoulders crouched inward like a scavenging vulture, and her hair was wiry and dry from lack of oil and care. Dark circles haloed her gaunt eyes from little sleep, and she couldn't remember when she'd last eaten.

She'd become addicted to the Twitter fight. The tug-of-war of rebutting the angry *isms*—racism, sexism, et cetera. Looking at herself, she felt both sad and strangely proud. A fierce and fearless female, she was. But she knew she couldn't continue like that. The exhilaration of heated debate would only lead her head-on into a brick wall of exhaustion. That's when she implemented her *wait until the storm passes; then and only then shall you proceed* policy.

It was hard, though. With the overturning of *Roe*, the country was ripping at the seams, and Twitter had no idea how invested Tye actually was. Caught in the middle of a powerful cultural firestorm, Tye stood in the center of the debate. She could rally the world if she wanted to. But instead, she just scratched her itching thumbs. *Wait until the storm passes; then and only then shall you proceed.*

"Babygal, come on here," Gran Izella called after her. "I smashed some Jiffy in your greens. You need to eat."

Tye smiled. Jiffy cornbread mix was against everything her gran Izella held dear. She believed in making her cornbread from scratch, by scrutinizing every grain of meal, buttermilk, egg, everything. Her corn muffins were part of what had made Rutabaga's such a hit in the early days. But Tye was the only person walking earth who hated them. So Gran Izella swallowed the pain, pride, and embarrassment of Jiffy Mix and made a separate pan for her favorite Babygal.

"I'm coming, Gran," Tye called to her. "Just a minute."

Tye burped mid-sentence. She could feel the acid creeping into her windpipe, and it made her gag uncontrollably. She clasped both hands around her mouth so Gran wouldn't hear her, but she was not in charge of her own impulses. Even so, she willed herself to breathe calm, slow breaths. She focused her energy toward her chest, up and down, in and out. Exhale pain and lack of control, and inhale the normal Tye. It had worked in hatha yoga, where the room's temperature could creep up to 110 degrees. It had worked while she ran her first half marathon. No reason why it shouldn't work during the first trimester of pregnancy. She closed her eyes. In and out, she thought. Up and down, she thought. And then she violently threw up a thick, yellow something.

"You okay in there, Babygal?" Izella asked from the kitchen. "You sound like a cat with a hair ball stuck."

"I'm good," Tye lied with as much authenticity as possible. "I'll be out in a minute."

"You lie worse than a puppy dog," Izella replied softly. "Come on out. Somebody wants to see you."

Tye unmuted Wendy Williams so Gran couldn't hear as clearly. She knelt down in front of the pool of yellow vomit. For breakfast, she'd had a few bites of toast, and for lunch a spoonful of broccoli casserole. She hadn't eaten anything yellow. She then took her index finger and tapped it to feel the texture. It looked and felt like an egg yolk, thick and kind of bouncy to the touch. That's when Tye began to cry.

Tye rarely cried. It wasn't that she'd been in denial; the magnitude of her predicament had hit her as soon as the pregnancy test read positive. Crying simply wasn't her way. She'd rather work than cry. Her boyfriend, Davis, was the opposite. Shouldered linebacker already recruited by the Falcons, Davis boo-hooed like a newborn. Cornfed country-boy Davis and nose-in-a-book intellect Tye, they'd been together since fifth grade, and it was love, absolutely.

She'd only missed one damn week of birth control. One damn week. And they'd only had sex once within that one damn week. It had been enough, though. Another thing Tye itched to tweet about. Though she knew they'd call her a slut for getting pregnant. Or a disappointment. Or a missed opportunity. Or a sad, sad case. None of that hurt. Actually, it energized her.

What truly hurt was her loss of control.

Tye: that badass with the Twitter fingers.

Tye: that fabulous girl with the sick butt-length braids and quick wit.

Tye: that female who could take down a powerful senator with a single Tweet.

Tye: that yogi who mastered the headstand, camel, and cobra poses within the span of a single class.

Tye: the youngest girl to complete the Decatur Half Marathon in under two hours and fifteen minutes.

That was Tye prior to throwing up the egg yolk. Tye now couldn't even control the foreign substance expelling itself from her own body. No breathing exercises or willpower could make it stop. In that moment, she recognized that her body, and her life, were no longer her own. She belonged to the thing growing inside her, and a bunch of cloaked men said she couldn't eliminate it.

Applause roared from the television set. Wendy Williams was welcoming her first guest on set, Stevie J from *Love and Hip Hop*. Tye's eyes welled up even more watching him walk from backstage to join Wendy for an interview. Stevie J was a musical genius. A multi-instrumentalist musician who wrote some of America's most iconic pieces for some of the best singers in modern history. He was a Mozart, but no one cared about that. All anyone cared about was Stevie J's relationship with Joseline, and how many kids he had, and how much back child support he owed, and how much drama he could rile up on his reality show. It was a tragedy, Tye thought, and she could end up exactly like him—a brilliant, uniquely talented hot mess. Then she shook off the thought, turned off the television, and tore off an obscene amount of paper towels to clean up her own vomit.

That wouldn't be her fate. No. She wouldn't allow herself to become a statistic of teen pregnancy. No. She needed a plan. A method of action to tackle the seemingly untackleable, just like she'd done with yoga and the marathon and social media.

"Tye," a voice that wasn't Gran Izella's said after a small knock. "Open up." Poised, serene, almost musical in its melody, it was the unmistakable voice of Nana Sue.

"I'm here, too, my heart," said Grandma Sippi. "Came soon as we heard."

Anger filled Tye's body. How could Gran decide to tell SIS without asking her first? It was a rousing betrayal. A lack of loyalty. Now she'd have to sit across from three women who had no idea what she was going through. Three perfect women—Nana Sue, an accomplished curator; Gran Izella, owner of the most successful diner in the ATL; and Grandma Sippi, world's most loving grandmother and prayer queen of Valdosta. It should've been her choice who knew, just like it should've been her choice if she kept it.

She flung the door open, readying herself for a rare argument with Gran Izella. But she wasn't there; no one was.

"Hello?" asked Tye, careening around the doorway. "Where are y'all?"

"Dining room," said the three ladies at once.

When Tye laid eyes on them, all anger left. They were the most beautiful sight—strong, wise, welcoming women with no judgment anywhere on them. Tye sat across from them and became a timid child in the presence of queens.

"You go first, Sue," Izella said with tears in her smiling eyes. Tye had never seen Gran Izella cry before. It wasn't her way.

"Tyesha, my love," Sue started. "I've missed your beautiful face."

"I . . ." Tye said, but Gran Izella held her hand in the air.

"You, child, are to sit quietly until we all have our turns to speak," Gran Izella said in a tone not to be questioned. "Understand?"

Tye nodded.

Nana Sue began telling the story of how her daughter, Katherine, came into the world. She told a story of melody and music eclipsed by silence. Sue kept making a point to say how much she loved her daughter, but the cost was high. In her opinion, too high for her seventeen-year-old mind and body. Nana Sue sang a song of thick regret of what could have come of her without giving birth to Katherine so early in life.

Grandma Sippi went second. Her tiny hands flailing as she spoke. She told the tale of a lonely girl as if it were not herself. A girl in a small house with a good book and a good papa. Vulnerable to nasty men, she said. A girl so much smaller than you are now, she told Tye. Less learned. More hopeful. A dreamer who brought two dreams to life in a tiny apartment building high up in Chicago surrounded by the purest love. Grandma Sippi sang a song of gratitude to God for bringing her through the darkness and out into the sunshine.

As Sippi spoke, Sue began to cry without control, and Izella, too. They clasped onto one another to make up one flesh, and when they let go, all eyes fell on Izella.

"You haven't touched your Jiffy, Babygal," she said.

Tye knew her. She saw something inside her that was hidden so deep that bringing it up might kill her. Gran Izella was terrified of whatever that thing was. Terrified. Nana Sue and Grandma Sippi sensed it, too. They changed the subject.

"Back then, we had no choice, you see?" said Grandma Sippi. "I can't say that I could've gone through with something like that if I could've, but a choice would've been a good thing. I was a child myself. A clueless one, to boot."

"I would have done it," Nana Sue said with zero doubt. "I love Katherine more than life, but that father of hers is a jackass."

Nana Sue and Grandma Sippi laughed out, seemingly relieved to have spoken their truths aloud. A lightness came over them. But Gran Izella was growing heavier by the moment.

"I had a sister," Gran Izella said, bringing the laughter to an unnatural halt. "A beautiful sister named . . ." Izella looked off into nothing. "I don't dare say her name. Sippi, say it."

"Ola," Grandma Sippi said without hesitation. "Her name . . . was Ola."

"Ola Mae Murphy," added Nana Sue with a reassuring smile.

Izella smiled at them, grateful. "She was having a boy. Probably a boy named Walter Jr., suffice to say. No choice back then, like Sippi said. No choice, so we made the choices ourselves. Just us girls. Little girls making big-girl choices. And no way on God's green earth I'm letting you, Tyesha, go through this same shit alone. SIS is with you. Well . . ." Izella stood and began to clean Tye's untouched collards and Jiffy. "We better put this up before it gets cold."

"Can I ask," Tye began. "What happened to Ola?"

"I killed her." Gran Izella's face showed no emotion, but the plate she held tilted from left to right like a seesaw. Nana Sue leaped for it before she dropped it completely. "I was the stupid one who thought I was smart enough to help, and I killed her."

Sippi and Sue led Izella back to the table, and they honed in on one another. Tye disappeared to them as they fell into a long talk about life and choice. Still, Tye felt proud to listen to three powerful women who'd once been just like her—powerless. No control over which way their lives went. Forced to choose for themselves while the boys and men went on to lead companies and congresses and courts that chose for them.

How many women have gone through this? Tye thought. How many still are? Silently and alone.

Fuck that, she thought before quietly picking up her phone to open Twitter to write a stream of consciousness poem. Her thumbs took on life.

THREAD

to my followers: yesterday, while sitting in the waiting room at an abortion clinic, I found out my right to rid my

body of this unwanted pregnancy was taken away. I've got a full ride to Harvard next year. Wtf am I supposed to do with a baby?

how many girls have gone thru this? how many of our mothers & grandmothers have dealt w/ this sht throughout history? how many girls have to die b4 the rest of us wake the fuck up? HOW MANY GIRLS R OUT THERE JUST LIKE ME?

fast girls,

slow girls,

rich girls,

poor girls.

lit girls,

it girls,

no girls,

know girls.

broke girls,

fixed girls,

nick's girls,

jack's girls,

ted's girls,

dead girls,

loud-mouthed girls to speak for the girls who don't know how,

quiet-lipped girls who hold their words for max impact,

traumatized girls,

open up your eyes, Girls,

do you a twirl, Girl,

change the fucking world, Girl! #girlslikeus

SEND

AUTHOR'S NOTE

Life is a circle. Many iterations in the English language attempt to make these four words sound more profound—what goes around comes around, there's nothing new under the sun, history repeats itself. In the end, it all means the same thing—life, in fact, is a circle, and these four words sum up the real reason I wrote this novel.

As one of my resolutions for a wise life, I intentionally gravitate toward the eldest person in the room. To illuminate the invisible pitfalls at the feet of society, I want to hear the eighty-year-old woman's perspective. I want to hear about how things used to be in all veins of life—socially, economically, politically. I want to approach her and ask, *Where did you step, madam? Do you regret stepping there? If so, lead me to that particular spot so that I may avoid it.*

I've never been turned away, not once in my life, and I've asked a lot of seniors a lot of questions. Our elders are more than willing to share this merry-go-round called history, but dear Lord, no one is listening. Usually, when I approach them at the bus stop, or in a restaurant, or at the family reunion, they've been left alone to sit comfortably with their brilliant insights still stuck inside their time-wise heads. Then, enter me.

Bring on the four-hour breakdown of World War Two, I say, and help me understand what the '40s really felt like. The '60s, too. I want it all, madam. Where were you when Nixon resigned? When Martin Luther King Jr. gave his rousing speech on the steps of the Lincoln Memorial? And when Roe v. Wade became law? Did it penetrate into your social consciousness? Or was it just another piece of legislation? What was life like *before Roe* became law? The answer to the latter question led to the inevitable topic of backwoods abortion.

I grew up in the southern United States, and most of my elders were black women raised in the outskirts of Birmingham, Alabama, and Atlanta, Georgia. These women were champions to me, but their faces twisted with pain at the topic of backwoods abortion. They had known, or known of, someone who died in those backwoods, and the death of an unwed black girl didn't make the evening news.

Back then, unmarried pregnant black girls sat at the bottom of the bottomless pit of judgment with zero hope of rising out of it. The lucky ones had at least one supportive family member to help them navigate their predicament, but most were tossed aside as soiled human beings. In a small town filled with such antagonism, a girl could get desperate. And at the core of desperation rests a dangerous lack of restraint, which, in many cases, came in the form of wire hangers, homemade concoctions, and female death.

There's no way to know how many young women died in the backwoods, but regardless of political stance on the law itself, Roe v. Wade eliminated a fair amount of that death through safer options. I know this from the mouths of those who lived through it, many of whom are still living to tell the tale to anyone who cares to hear it.

One particular pregnant black girl who died in the backwoods inspired the writing of this novel. I will never reveal her name or the person who told me about her, but I've known her my whole life. Intangible her. The ghost of her, staring at the clear blue sky before dying in her mother's arms a few hours later. The ripple her death created within her nuclear family and her neighborhood still exists today. And unbeknownst to any of them, that ripple eventually morphed into the tsunami inside me called *Girls Like Us*.

Still, I toiled with whether to release this book. The concept lived in the notes of my iPhone for many years. And the original draft was an intentionally detached contemporary tale relating in no way to the girl who inspired it. Then, in the summer of 2018, the Supreme Court flipped, and I thought, life is indeed a circle.

I scrapped the majority of what I'd written and rewrote the whole novel as historical fiction. The voices of my elders helped me along in writing this book, too many to name here.

Today, the pendulum swings dangerously close to those backwoods. And if life is a circle, the string that holds the heavy weight of the law could snap under societal pressure. Leading so many choiceless girls back to 1972.